RED PARDEE

PHILIP KETCHUM

SAGEBRUSH
Large Print Westerns

First published in the United States by Ballantine

First Isis Edition
published 2021
by arrangement with
Golden West Literary Agency

A catalogue record for this book is available
from the British Library.

ISBN 978–1–78541–871–6

Published by
Ulverscroft Limited
Anstey, Leicestershire

Set by Words & Graphics Ltd.
Anstey, Leicestershire
Printed and bound in Great Britain by
TJ Books Ltd., Padstow, Cornwall

This book is printed on acid-free paper

CHAPTER
ONE

Colonel Tarkington sat at his desk in the headquarters office at Fort Apache, studying the paper in his hand. He was sure it was not in proper form, though to be truthful, he was not sure what the proper form was. On that basis, he could deny Gallard's petition. He felt that he ought to deny it, but there was another consideration to be weighed: he wanted to get rid of the boy. Washington wanted that too. In that case it might be best to make a practical decision.

Gallard, who was watching the colonel across the desk, cleared his throat, then leaned forward and said, "I didn't know what to do. The newspaper said that anybody who wanted the boy and could look after him, should make a petition to the commanding officer at Fort Apache; but I wasn't sure what a petition was. I asked a lawyer in Dry Fork how to make a petition and he said to put in a letter what I would do for the boy. That's what I did."

"It's a very good letter," Tarkington said. "Do you really mean to do all the things you listed?"

"Why not?"

"I just wondered. Do you want to see the boy?"

"Yes I do."

Tarkington got to his feet, walked to the door and called his orderly. He said, brusquely, "Go find the Indian boy. Bring him here." Then he walked back to his desk, sat down.

"Why did you say he was an Indian?" Gallard asked.

"He's half Indian, half white, you know," Tarkington said. "A breed. His father was Jacques Pardee, a scout, trapper, and a friend of the Indians, but one day they killed him. The boy's mother was an Indian squaw. He'll probably tell you his mother was the daughter of a chief, but I wouldn't bet on it."

"How old is he? The newspaper said . . ."

"He's fourteen. His father was killed almost three years ago. Since then the boy has been in the hands of the Apaches and I don't think they were easy on him. Look at his back some day; it's scarred from beatings. He was thin, half starved when we got him. He's still thin."

"How did you get him?"

"In the last treaty we signed with the Apaches, among other things, they agreed to the return of all captives. There were only a few. The boy was one of them. I think one of the reasons he was included was that they didn't want him."

"They could have killed him if they didn't like him."

"This might have been worse, to hand him over to the white men. Most whites figure that a breed is the same as an Indian. You ought to know that yourself."

"It's a big country," Gallard said. "There ought to be enough room for everyone."

"Do you have any children?" Tarkington asked.

"Had one. He's gone." Gallard scowled, hesitated, then motioned vaguely with both hands. "It's kind of lonely, down the valley. My wife and I thought it might be a good idea to have someone around."

"Don't you plan to work him?"

"Certainly, I explained that in the letter. But that's not the most important thing."

Tarkington started to speak, but he held back. He had been about to say that back home, in the east, there were hundreds of orphans who needed homes. If it was up to him he would never take a chance on a breed. But then he remembered he wanted to get rid of the boy, and in view of that, it was foolish to be critical.

He took another look at Gallard. He was short, stocky, middle aged, and he looked husky enough to take care of himself. He had dark eyes, a square-set jaw, and there were a good many lines on his face. Maybe he knew what he was doing in taking on a chore like this. He had decided to approve the man's petition.

There was a knock on the door and he called, "Yes? What is it?"

"Sergeant Beck, sir." The answer was muffled. "Here's the Injun boy, sir."

"Send him in," Tarkington said.

The door opened and a boy stepped inside. He was tall for fourteen, thin, and he stood very straight. His hair was black and it hung to his shoulders. A headband held it down. The eyes were black. In Tarkington's opinion, the eyes were too bold, too defiant. The boy's skin was a dark brown but some of the coloring might

3

have come from the sun and the wind. His clothes were old, not at all suitable.

"This is Mr. Gallard," Tarkington said, and he motioned that way. "He thinks he might have a home for you. How would you like that?"

The boy took a quick look at Gallard, but he said nothing.

"He can talk," Tarkington said, "but mostly he doesn't. The troopers call him Red. They say that's his name."

"I'm not sure about that," Gallard said. "What would you like to be called, son?"

The boy moistened his lips. "Red."

"You mean it?" Gallard said. "Is that what you want to be called?"

"Yes." The boy nodded. "That is my name. It is what my father called me."

"Then we sure won't change it," Gallard said. "Red Pardee. Come to think about it, that's a pretty good name."

It was very warm in the headquarters office, but it had been hotter in the stable where Red had worked. Here, it smelled better, too. And what was happening was interesting. Since he had been brought here, four months ago, nothing had happened. The work he had done, the necessary bathings, the insults of the troopers, things like that were not worth thinking about But to go somewhere else, he might like that very much. It had been better at the fort than when he had been with the Apaches, but not much better. He hadn't

4

liked the Apaches, but neither did he like the troopers. If he could live in the mountains again . . .

"Red?" It was Gallard who was talking. "Would you like to hear what I have suggested to Colonel Tarkington?"

He nodded. "Yes."

"I am proposing that you work for me for the next five years," Gallard said. "I will give you room and board, and the first year you work for me I will pay you fifteen dollars a month; the second year, twenty dollars a month; the third year, twenty-five dollars a month; and the fourth and fifth years, thirty dollars a month. In addition, my wife will teach you lettering so you can read and write and she will teach you how to do sums. For the first three years we will pay for your clothing. In return, you will work for us, do whatever we ask, within reason. Does that sound fair?"

Red looked toward the window. He was not sure about that but there were other things to think about. He turned back to look at Gallard. "Do you live in the mountains?"

"No." The man shook his head. "But the mountains aren't very far away, less than a day's ride."

"Will I have a horse?"

"Any of several horses."

"Will I have a gun?"

"Yes. I'll teach you how to handle it."

Colonel Tarkington interrupted. "I don't know about that, Gallard, I'm not sure that's the wise thing to do."

"What else should I do?" Gallard asked. "This is frontier country."

"But to put a gun in the hands of an Indian . . ."

"He won't be an Indian."

"He's a breed. That's the same thing. If you put a gun in his hands a lot of folks won't like it."

"A lot of folks don't like a lot of things," Gallard said. "I figure it's a practical thing to teach Red how to handle himself."

"And I still don't like it," Tarkington said. "I approve most things you outlined. You have offered the boy more than you should. But this about guns . . ."

"Where do you come from, Colonel?"

"Arlington, Virginia."

"That's across from Washington, a nice, quiet town. You don't have to wear guns back there, but this is 1871 in the Territory of Arizona, and out here, men wear them, depend on them, live by them. That's how things are."

"I still don't have to like it," Tarkington said.

Red had listened to part of what had been said, but not to everything. The important things had already been mentioned: he would live near the mountains, he would have a horse, and he would have a gun. Those last two things were supremely important. Even when he had been a captive of the Apaches he had looked forward to these two things. When he had been brought to the fort he had been closer to a horse and a gun, a horse and a gun of his own. Now it seemed he was almost there. Gallard had said so.

He was saying, now, "Well, Colonel? How about it? Is the petition all right? Can you approve it?"

"I can endorse it," Tarkington said. "I'll have to send it in to the War Department for approval, but I have a feeling there won't be much of an argument. I'm not going to mention the matter of the gun."

"Thanks, Colonel."

"You know, this Indian trouble isn't all over. There'll be more of it."

"Not everywhere," Gallard said. "There won't be trouble when people learn to get along with each other."

"Some never will."

"Could be you're right," Gallard said, and he stood up. "Can I take the boy now? The day's only half over. I could cut down on the next two days' drive if we get started this afternoon."

"Sure. Go ahead."

"You ready, son?"

Red nodded, and then for the first time he really looked at Gallard. He was short, and wrinkled like his father. He had a measured way of saying things, and that was also like his father, and he thought: "I must be very careful about this man. I must not like him too much for someday I might have to kill him."

They left shortly after noon, riding in a light farm wagon pulled by a team. Tom Gallard was driving, Red sat beside him. In the bed of the wagon there were several folded blankets, a folded piece of canvas, several jugs of water, and two wooden boxes. There was a rifle in the seat, behind them, and in addition, Gallard was wearing a holstered hand gun.

7

Red had not said a word. He seemed tense, on edge. Gallard, wondered what to say in order to make him feel more at ease, and after thinking about it, he asked, "You hungry?"

"I am always hungry," Red answered.

"Then climb back into the bed of the wagon," Gallard said. "You'll see two boxes. That's where the food is. See what you can find. There ought to be some cooked meat wrapped in a wet cloth. There's a knife with it. Cut me a piece, and you can have the rest. There's some cheese and bread and jelly, too. Help yourself to anything."

Red climbed into the bed of the wagon. He started exploring the two boxes. Gallard looked back once, but that was all. He hoped he was doing the right thing in taking this boy with him. He hoped he would be able to get along with him. He hoped the boy would like his wife, and that Myrt would like him. That was awfully important.

He was scowling by this time. He had mentioned to several people in Dry Fork what he was going to do, and almost everyone had warned him not to. If he wanted to take on an orphan, he should send away for one, write to some orphanage; get a white boy, not a breed. It was Myrt who had noticed the story in the newspaper about the boy who was being held at Fort Apache. And she had said, right away, "Why don't we take him, Tom. Someone ought to." She had been in favor of it from the beginning, and even after three of their neighbors had warned them against him. Myrt was a strong woman, all right She had not changed her mind. Nor had he changed his mind, after he decided that someone ought to give the boy a chance. So he had gone ahead. Now he was hoping he had not made a mistake.

He felt a touch on his shoulder and he turned. Red was holding out a piece of the meat, a generous portion. Gallard reached for it, nodded, and said, "Thanks. Did you save enough for yourself?"

"Yes."

"Find something else," Gallard said. "Eat all you want to, but remember — we might not be able to get a rabbit for supper."

"Will you use the rifle?"

"Have to."

"Can I shoot the rifle?"

"Think you could do that?"

"I would like to try."

"We'll see about it," Gallard said. "After you finish eating you can drive the team. It's not hard. The team will stay on the road, but they know it if there's a hand on the reins. Now and then you'll have to touch the horses with the whip. I said, touch them. That's all you have to do."

Red nodded. He was still eating, and his mouth was full. That might have been the reason he was silent.

Gallard chewed on the meat, peered ahead. He was fifty-three, and he could have boasted that he was an oldtimer in this part of the country. He and Myrt had moved west sixteen years ago, in the spring of fifty-five. They had settled, first, in Tucson. That had been their home for eleven years, although he had been away a good part of the time. He had prospected for gold, had worked as a range rider, had been a stagecoach driver, and guard. He had even served as a scout for the army. He and Myrt had done fairly well, financially, but they had not been very successful with their son. Five years ago, when the boy was just twenty, he had been arrested as an outlaw and sent to prison. After that, he and Myrt had moved to the valley below Dry Fork. That was where they were headed now.

Red climbed back into the seat beside him. Gallard handed him the reins. Then for a time, he talked about the team and how to handle them. And he talked about horses in general, what they were like. Red seemed to listen but Gallard was not sure whether he was listening or not. His son had been like that; he had seemed to listen.

They camped that night, drove on the next day, camped when it got dark, then drove on soon after dawn. Red did most of the driving. He enjoyed it. He had learned how to unhitch the team and how to put them in harness again. He had learned how to rub the horses down. More important, he had been permitted to shoot the rifle several times. He had not been very accurate but he was just starting.

"Look around, Red," Gallard said as they started the third morning. "Notice the country. This is where you'll be living."

They were out of the mountains. The land around them was mostly flat but there were hills and gulleys here and there. There were mesquite thickets, tangles of chaparral, clumps of junipers, and everywhere the Saguaro stood like sentinels. The grass looked wiry and there was too much cactus.

"I like the mountains better," he said bluntly.

"Maybe you do," Gallard said, "but keep watching. We're dropping into a widening valley. The grass will turn better. After a time we'll come to a tree-lined river and you'll be noticing cattle along the way. Some of them belong to me. They will become part of your responsibility, but don't worry about that now."

"Are we almost home?" Red asked.

"We ought to make it by noon."

He frowned. The ride had not been bad. Gallard had been no problem to him. He was stern, but not in a hard way, and he thought he could get along with him. But he was less sure about his wife, the woman he called Myrt. Gallard seemed to like her and maybe she was all right, but he was not sure about that. He would have to wait and see what she was like. For some reason, he was uneasy about her.

Far up ahead but off to the side was a stirring cloud of dust. It seemed to be moving this way.

He pointed to it. "Look."

"Several riders, I think," Gallard said. "We'll be able to tell in a minute or two."

Red kept watching, and gradually, through the dust, he could make out a number of mounted men, headed this way. Five mounted men, no — there were six.

He glanced at Gallard. The man was frowning. He touched his holstered gun as though to make sure it was still there, and he did another thing — he moved his rifle to where he could reach it easier. And after a moment he said, "This is just what we don't need."

He didn't explain what that meant.

Red kept driving the team but his muscles had tightened up. He could guess that the men, riding this way, represented some kind of danger.

"When those men get near," Gallard said, "we'll stop the wagon. I'll do the talking. Understand?"

Red nodded, but he meant only that he would be silent. He had no idea what this was all about.

"That's Ben Justine, riding this way," Gallard said. "He's got five of his men with him. He's got a place here in the valley. I don't get along with him very well. We've got — different ways of looking at things. Too bad we ran into him."

Red kept driving the team. He looked ahead, watched the approaching men. They were almost here.

"You can stop the wagon now," Gallard said.

Red pulled on the reins, stopped the wagon, then he waited, staring straight ahead. The muscles of his face had hardened. His expression would not change while the men were here.

The men were pulling up on Gallard's side of the wagon, and right away, one of the men spoke. Red caught a glimpse of him out of the corner of his eye. The man was big, heavy, wide shouldered. He had a black beard and a dark, scowling face. His voice was harsh. "Is that the Injun kid?"

"He's half white," Gallard said mildly.

"That don't count, an' you know it."

"It does as far as I'm concerned. Anything else, Justine?"

The man leaned forward in the saddle. "You mean to keep him?"

"Sure do."

"Then keep him outa my part of the country."

"What's your part of the country? This is open range."

Justine shook his head, then for a moment he seemed to be glaring at the boy next to Gallard. Red was aware of that, but he didn't move. He sat very straight, his head high, and there might have been a hint of defiance in his attitude.

Gallard spoke again. "Just leave the boy alone, Justine. If you want to pick on someone, try someone your own size — like me."

The man took a quick, sharp breath, and he said, "Some day I will. I will sooner, if you don't keep that Injun kid outa my way."

"I said, leave him be," Gallard said, and there was an edge in his voice.

There was half a minute of silence, a tense half minute. Several of the other men had moved, spread away from Justine, but nothing happened, and after another moment Justine made a sound in his throat and then said, "By God, you go too far. You'll hear more about this, Gallard."

"Sure," Gallard said. "Sure."

Justine lifted the reins of his horse, wheeled away and rode off. His five men trailed him. Not one had said a word.

"We can move on," Gallard said, and he seemed to have relaxed. "You can start the team."

Red did that, and when the team was slow starting he used the whip, but he used it lightly, the way Gallard had suggested.

"That sounded like it was all about you," Gallard said, "but it wasn't. Justine doesn't like you. You're half white, half Indian, a breed. There's nothing shameful about that and certainly, it's not your fault, but because you're not like he is, he dislikes you. So he said some things about you but he was really hitting at me. He doesn't like me at all. Do you understand what I'm talking about?"

Red shook his head. "That black-bearded man, he talked like the troopers at the fort."

"Sure. He's like them. He doesn't like you because you're part Indian. But for other reasons, he doesn't like me, and a good part of his anger is aimed at me. I guess I mean that you're not alone, being hated. I'm right there with you."

"You're not part Indian," Red said.

"Nope. I got in the way of some things Justine wanted, and for those reasons, he hates me. All the hate in the world is not reserved to you. You'll find it in a good many other places. A man is never cut off from the world unless he does that himself. Maybe you don't understand me."

Red wasn't sure that he did. He thought about the black-bearded Justine. Some day he would face him, stand right up to him, tell him who he was, and then ask him what he meant to do about it. Before then, of course, he had to learn how to handle a gun. In fact, that was the most important thing in the world.

He looked at Gallard. "When can I have a gun?"

"There are a lot of things that come before that," Gallard said. "We need new clothes for you, we have to set up a program of schooling. You must learn to ride a horse, learn how to care for it. And learn about cattle. With everything else, you'll learn how to handle a gun. It all runs together, Red. Growing up and learning to be a man covers a lot of territory."

A stony expression settled down on Red's face. It seemed that the white man's world was filled with too many unnecessary things.

CHAPTER
TWO

It took Red more then two years to decide what he thought about Myrt Gallard. He started by ignoring her as much as he could, treating her as though she was unimportant. That didn't work very well. He tried being quietly antagonistic. For a time he hated her, but he couldn't keep on hating her. She never hit back, she was never unpleasant, and she had an endless amount of patience. It occurred to him one day that he had never looked at her honestly. She knew an awful lot of things; when she said something it was usually important, and if he didn't listen he missed something. This schooling he was getting was for him. It was not for her. It didn't add to her, it added to him. It had nothing to do with guns or fighting but there were other things in the world. Many other things.

There were other towns than Dry Fork. She told him about them. There were other lands, there were other people. There was such a thing as time, and distance, and there was a way of measuring them. There was a thing called numbers, sums, addition and subtraction. There were names for grasses, plants, shrubs and trees. There were other metals than gold and iron. There was an animal kingdom. There were other things to be learned in books. Myrt Gallard had made him learn to read. She had opened a new world to him. He no longer hated her, and he thought, "From now on I'll think about her the way I remember my mother, but I will never tell her this. She wouldn't understand."

His feelings toward Tom Gallard had also changed. In the beginning he had meant to use him, but as time went on he had to pay the man a grudging respect. He was bluntly honest. He could be stern and unbending. If Red was forgetful, Gallard reminded him. If he made a mistake, Gallard pointed it out. He had thought there was a softness in the man but he discovered that if there were any soft points in him, anywhere, they were all for Myrt. Not for him and not for the world.

Red had learned how to use a hand gun, how to whip it out of his holster and how to fire it, quickly and accurately. He had learned how to use a rifle, how to sight it, and how to allow for the strength of the wind.

He was learning another thing — how to use his fists. This was a continuing lesson, repeated again and again. Red had been startled when it began. His first lesson came the first month he was here. Gallard had led him around the barn late one afternoon, and had stopped and said, "You like handling a gun, don't you?"

"I have to," Red answered.

"But you also like it."

"Yes."

"I thought so," Gallard said, "but that's not good. I want you to practice with your gun. I want you to become one of the best, but I don't want you to have to depend on your gun. You'll be growing up before long. You'll be your own man, and when you move out in the world you'll find that most men can settle their problems by bargaining, by give-and-take, by agreement. Sometimes a fight can't be avoided, but you don't always have to use your gun. Men fight in another way — with their fists. I want you to learn to use your fists. Do you know what I mean?"

"I think so," Red said.

"Hmmm. I hope so," Gallard said, "because this is going to be a little rough. I'm bigger than you, so to begin with I'll only use one hand, an open hand. You can use both fists. Are you ready?"

Red stared at the man, wide-eyed. "You mean I should . . ."

"Like this," Gallard said.

His hand whipped out, slapped across Red's face. The blow was hard enough to stagger him.

"Now, brace yourself, and then bore in," Gallard said. "See what you can do with your fists. Try to knock me off my feet."

Gallard's hand slapped at him again, hard. It almost knocked Red off his feet, but that was enough to start him. He recovered, and he plowed in at Gallard, pumping his fists. He didn't aim at anything, he just hit, and mostly he hit the air. Then he started trying to hit Gallard's face but the man kept moving his head. Red couldn't reach it. A hard slap across his face knocked him to his knees but he got up right away, and charged in.

18

That happened again and again. He would drive in, slam his fists at Gallard's head, but after a moment a slap would knock him down and he would have to get up again, and lunge in, only to get knocked down again.

How many times that happened he would never know, but he kept trying. He kept trying until he couldn't get up. At that point he might have looked whipped, but inside he was raging. Right then, he would have liked to kill Tom Gallard.

The man stood above him, grinning, and he said, "Hmmm, you're pretty good. You didn't quit. I like that about you. You'll do better next time."

Red glared at the man — at least, he tried to.

"I told you this was going to be a little rough," Gallard said, "but there's no sense making it easy. In a fight you get hurt. If you're good with your fists and stop it early, you don't get hurt so badly. You know, one of these days you'll give me a bloody nose."

"I will do more than that," Red said. He was still panting for air. He felt a little dizzy.

"We'll try this every month," Gallard said. "We'll keep on doing this until I have to use both hands, then one fist and then both. We won't stop until you can knock me off my feet. Think that will ever happen?"

Red was sitting up. He said, "Yes. It will happen sooner than you think."

"Hmmm. We'll see about that," Gallard said. "Come on, get up on your feet. Time to clean up."

In the first three years Red spent with the Gallards, he changed a great deal. He had grown taller, heavier, and he was more sure of himself as a person. He had become a good rider. He had come to know cattle and he knew how to handle them. He was amazingly good with a rifle and probably no one but Gallard knew how good he was with a hand gun. He had become fond of Myrt and he got along with Gallard, most of the time. They still had their monthly fist fight. It had become a limited contest — fifteen minutes by the clock. If they'd let it go longer someone might have been hurt, and as Gallard said, this was a learning session. In fifteen minutes, two grown men could do a lot of damage, and Red, at least in size and weight, had become a man. At seventeen he was six feet tall, and he weighed a hundred and fifty pounds. He was thin, but all bone and muscle.

Red got along with the Gallards pretty well, and things were getting better. How the other people in the valley and in the town felt about him was more complicated. He was a halfbreed, and because of that a good many people instinctively disliked him. Some might change, some never would. Then, Tom Gallard had a certain amount of standing in the valley. People liked him. He seemed unafraid of Justine and that was important. Because of that, because the small ranchers needed him, maybe they could overlook the halfbreed boy he had brought into his home.

As far as Red was concerned, besides the Gallards he had no friends at all. Among the valley and the town people, there were some who hated him because of his Indian blood, and all the rest disliked him, and distrusted him, but would put up with him out of respect to the Gallards, or out of their own Christian beliefs, whatever those were.

Red seldom went to town alone. If he had to get something he might ride in, get it, and ride out. He wouldn't stay; there was too much chance of trouble. In three years he had seen Justine maybe a dozen times. The man never looked at him, never saw him. There were others like that, people who knew him but never spoke to him unless they had to. For them, apparently, he didn't exist. Of course if the Gallards were with him some of these people might smile at him, stiffly. People like that he almost hated.

If Red had been friendly things might have been different. Or partly different. But he had not been friendly. If anyone else but the Gallards were around he became stiff, and silent, and he couldn't smile. Maybe everyone didn't hate him, or dislike him, but he thought they did. And he had developed another enemy, he was sure of that: Chet Ingerhall, the son of Mike and Jolly Ingerhall, neighbors and friends of the Gallards. Because of that friendship Red regretted what had happened. If he'd been able to, he would have avoided the trouble he ran into, and it might have been possible to do that if he had backed off, run, but it seemed wrong to try that.

Chet was several years older than he was, but they were about the same size. They had met several times, casually, and there had been no hard words. This time things were different. Red would never know why but it seemed to him that Chet deliberately tried to provoke the fight. Without any question, Chet started it.

The trouble was in the livery stable barn, in Dry Fork, one afternoon. The liveryman had been away. There had been no witnesses. It was a sudden fight, though it didn't last long. Chet might have fancied himself as pretty good with his fists, but against Red he didn't have a chance. Before he could land a single hard blow, he found himself on the ground. He got up and tried again, but he had no better success. The fifth time he went down he stayed.

Red was amazed at how easily he won. He knew he had learned a great deal from his battles with Gallard, but he couldn't believe he was as good as this. He had learned how to hit Gallard, but he had never been able to put him down. Maybe this victory over Chet didn't mean anything. Maybe Chet wasn't much of a fighter.

He looked down at the man at his feet. Chet's nose was bleeding, his lip was cut, and one eye was partly closed. He was breathing heavily but he didn't seem badly hurt. In a few minutes he would be able to get up and walk out, but what would happen then? What would Chet do, what would he say? He was cut and bleeding and he could claim he had been attacked suddenly before he could defend himself. Red could argue the matter, but who would believe him?

While he was puzzling over that Chet sat up, groaned, felt his head, then he started to get up and he managed it. He moved toward the door but stopped, and looked back at Red. He made a brief comment:

22

"Don't go away from here. We'll try this again. Next time I'll kill you."

He went outside, and as far as Red knew, Chet never said anything about what had happened in the barn. Maybe he had meant what he promised or maybe he had just said that.

Another year passed, Red's fourth year in the valley. He was eighteen now, a little taller, a little heavier, and in size a full-grown man. He had proved that he could spend a week in the saddle from dawn to dusk, but he seldom needed to because there was not that much work on the range. Part of the time he was in the fields with Gallard, or around the house. The barn had to be re-roofed, the well had to be deepened and walled. There were always home chores.

In the valley and centered in the town, there was a growing tension between black-bearded Justine and the other, smaller ranchers. Gradually, and over a period of time, Justine had taken over the western part of the valley. He bought out several ranches, squeezed out two others, and recently he had been putting pressure on two more places, the Thompsons' and the Broadwells'.

Red could tell that there was trouble ahead. Gallard looked worried, and Myrt did, too. Sometimes, in the evenings, they talked about what ought to be done, or what might be done. Myrt had suggested several times that they might sell out and go back to Tucson; if there was a range war, it was not worthwhile to try to stay. But she didn't say that very hopefully. She seemed to know that her husband did not mean to move.

23

Gallard came home from town late one afternoon, and said bluntly, "Helga Justine died a couple days ago."

"Oh, no," Myrt said. And then, "When is the funeral? We'll have to go."

"The funeral was held today. Justine didn't waste any time."

Myrt bit her lips. She was silent for a moment, then she asked, "What's going to happen now?"

"I don't know," Gallard said. "I always had the feeling that Helga was able to hold Justine back. Now we might find out if I was right."

Red listened to this, but he said nothing. He had heard of Justine's wife, but he had seen her only once. She had been a large woman and she had stood very straight. Her face had looked stern.

Myrt looked at him and said, "You wouldn't have liked her, Red. She was what we call a principled woman. She had her own ideas about right and wrong, and she fought hard for what she thought was right. To an extent, she ruled her husband. She was like that — but now she's dead. We are worried, now, that conditions in the valley might get worse." She paused, then she turned to Gallard. "What about Red?"

Gallard did not seem to have been listening. He asked, "What did you say, Myrt?"

"If there is going to be trouble, Mr. Justine might do something about Red. He's never liked him."

"Yes, he might." Gallard turned to Red. "How would you like to head for the mountains? You could spend a little time there, finishing the cabin we started."

Red was frowning. "I would rather stay here."

"What if I ordered you to go there?"

"I am not sure what I would do then. I am not afraid of Justine."

"I am," Gallard said. "I don't know what he'll do, how far he'll go. I don't know what's ahead. If I don't send you to the mountains will you stay around the house for a while? No trips up the valley alone. No trips to town."

"There are always things to do at home," Red said.

Gallard smiled. "Good. I think I'll stay home, myself."

Red left them, went outside, walked down to the creek and when he got there he turned and looked to the west, toward that part of the valley mostly controlled by Ben Justine. His face was impassive but inside his body his blood was churning madly. He seldom got excited but he was excited now. There was trouble ahead — trouble with Justine. That was just what he wanted, just what he had hoped for. This was why he had spent hours practicing with his hand gun and his rifle. This, really, was why he had learned how to handle his fists. He had been held back because of his heritage. He had been hindered from standing up against Justine because of his Indian blood, but since Justine was starting the trouble he had the right to defend himself — and he would do it in a way that people would never forget.

He might not be able to stay with the Gallards. He knew that, and he had prepared for such a time. He had set up three secret hideouts in the valley, and even stocked them with food. The one nearest here he had found three years ago. Another was far to the west, right in Justine's part of the valley. The third was off to the north; it was fairly new.

Red nodded quietly to himself. He was thinking: "Let the trouble come, and fast. Let it boil over. I have been waiting for this for a long time."

Gallard was silent for a time after Red left, then he turned to Myrt, and asked, "Was I wrong? Should I have sent him away?"

"He wouldn't have gone," Myrt answered. "After all, he's no longer a child."

"No. He's man size. If he had better judgment . . ."

"Give him time."

"There isn't more time, that's the trouble. If Justine decides to gobble up the valley, who's going to stop him?"

Myrt shook her head. "I didn't think he would . . . go that far."

"He could try it."

"What would happen? What would that start if he did?"

"I don't know, Myrt. I'm not sure what I'd do. We'll think about it." He got up and started for the door. "I'm going to see what Red's doing."

Red was down by the creek, just standing there, and Gallard didn't bother him. He walked past the barn, reached the slat-rail corral and hooked his arms on it. He looked at the horses but without seeing them. He was thinking of the possibilities ahead, and for him and for Myrt and for Red, nothing looked very good. He knew what a range war was like. He knew how quickly it could get started. He knew how much it hurt. And he knew who would get hurt the most. It would not be Justine's crowd, it would be the people of the valley, the ones not yet committed to fighting back. It would be the innocent ones, the ones who hoped to avoid a conflict, the ones who temporized — and then got smashed.

What should he do? There was no question about that. He ought to insist that they pack up tonight, and before dawn, head out of the valley. That was what he ought to do. And if he stayed . . .

He scowled and stared into the distance. Someone had to stand up to the Justines of the world and tell them to hold back. Someone had to get in the way. That was a sure way of getting hurt, and if you won your case you got little credit — but that was not the point. If you felt you had to take a stand, then that was what you did. You followed your conscience. That was a good rule to live by.

Two men came by the next night to see him, Ed Broadwell and Frank Thompson. Both were in their late thirties. Ed was short, stocky, had brown hair and a brown beard. Frank was taller, thinner, and had a persistent cough. He never looked well.

They reined up and tied their horses, and Gallard, from the doorway, noticed that their saddlebags were stuffed and each horse carried two fully loaded gunnysacks.

27

They came up to the door, nodded, and Ed said, "Gallard, can we see you for a minute?"

"Sure, come on in," Gallard said. Then he raised his voice, "Red, I want you to join us."

Both men seemed to hesitate. They were frowning as Red headed their way from the barn, where he had been working.

"Red is, kind of like a son," Gallard said. "I know you won't mind if he's with us."

"It's all right with me," Frank mumbled. "I've ridden with him."

Ed nodded, grunted.

They went inside, sat down. Myrt was there. She added more coffee and water to the coffee pot, shook up the fire, and joined them.

"Do you want me to tell the story?" Frank asked.

"Go ahead," Ed said.

"We sent our families away, yesterday," Frank said. "We did it sudden. We went to town. The stage to Santa Fe was almost empty. We packed our families in and then went home and waited. We waited at my house."

"Waited for what?" Gallard asked.

"Waited for Justine," Frank said. "He's been pushin' us hard, tryin' to buy us out. He said to me a week ago that if I didn't sell I'd probably lose every cow I had, lose 'em to rustlers. He didn't say so but his men would have done the rustlin'. He made the same speech to Ed Broadwell."

"It was a nastier speech," Ed said. "He told me I ought to sell an' move to a safe country — a place where my wife might not get hurt. He said there were a

28

lot of rough characters ridin' through the valley. Some day, while I was away, some of these characters might drop in on my wife. Nobody would be there to defend her. He made it clear what he meant."

Myrt's voice was low. "I can't believe it."

"That's what he said." Ed wiped his hand over his face. "I had to take it. Justine had two of his gunhawks with him. If I had started anything I wouldn't have lasted a minute. That's when I knew I had to send my wife and my two young sons away."

"What happend today?" Gallard asked.

"Ben Justine showed up, with five of his men," Frank answered. "Ed was with me. Justine heard in town about our families taking the stagecoach. He was sure we were ready to sell out. When we stalled, he damn near blew up. He gave us one more day to meet his terms, then he an' his men rode off."

"What were his terms?"

"Giveaway terms. A hundred dollars, cash; nine thousand nine hundred in six months, paid on demand at the bank in Dry Fork. We wouldn't live that long. We would never collect."

"And what would happen in another day, if you didn't meet Justine's terms?"

"He didn't say, and Ed and me decided we wouldn't hang around to find out what. We packed up some stuff an' headed out, geared for travelin'."

"Traveling where?" Gallard asked.

The two men looked at each other, shrugged, then Ed said, "Maybe you can tell us what we ought to do. We're not what you would call gunhawks but we know how to handle guns — an' we ain't about to give in to Ben Justine. If there's any way to hit back, then that's what we ought to do."

Gallard got up. He took a turn around the room, thinking. And another turn around the room, and still another. Myrt turned to the stove. She poured coffee for Frank and Ed, then she got three more cups, one for Red, one for Gallard, and one for herself.

Gallard stopped his pacing. He tried the coffee, then he started talking and he seemed to be thinking aloud. "This isn't the season to ship out cattle. If you two drop out of sight, your cattle most likely won't be bothered. That's in your favor. Of course, your houses might accidentally burn down. You've got to count on that."

"By god, we'll turn bushwhacker," Frank said.

"That's a quick way to die," Gallard said. "The average man would get run down."

"Then what are we gonna do?"

"Where did your families go?"

"They all went to Ed's relatives."

"Sure," Ed said. "Don't worry about the folks. What about us?"

"Do you know the mountains north of here?"

"I've been there," Frank said.

"I have sort of a cabin in the mountains, north of here," Gallard said. "It's not finished, but you could camp there. I can tell you how to get there."

"But why'd we want to go there?"

"Maybe you don't," Gallard said. "But you've come here for advice and that's all I can suggest. Go there

30

and wait for a time, until we can see what's going to happen in the valley. We need to wait and see what Justine is going to do."

"I can tell you that now," Frank said. "He wants the whole damned valley."

"Then he'll move against someone else, York, or Weiler, or me. We'll see what happens. Give us two weeks."

Ed shook his head. "You mean we gotta sit an' wait for two whole weeks? I don't like waitin'."

"No one does," Gallard said. "Go and fight Justine alone — or back off and wait until others are ready to join you. Play it smart, this time. Wait until we can see Justine's hand."

Frank nodded slowly. "You know, that might be a good idea. You want us to step out of sight for a couple of weeks."

"I want you to head for the mountains, and stay there where I can find you, until I send for you. Two weeks — or it might be less."

Frank nodded again, then Ed did, and Gallard thought: "I can't get out of it, now. I'm committed to whatever is ahead. Right now I'm in a shadow fight, but it won't be long before the trouble comes out in the open."

He could count on Myrt, he knew, and he could count on these two men. He glanced at Red, and for a moment he could see past his usually impassive face. He looked almost excited, eager for whatever was ahead. He was even breathing faster.

He caught just that glimpse of how Red felt, then the look was gone. But that was enough. He was not going to have to worry about Red.

CHAPTER
THREE

Ben Justine was forty-eight years old. In his own opinion he was in the prime of life, a big man, physically powerful. He could stay in the saddle all day and not be overly tired at night. He could sit up all night playing poker or he could spend the night with a woman, and show no ill effects in the morning. He knew how to handle his fists. He could challenge anyone in a rough and tumble fight. He slept well, he ate well, he was building up his ranch. In every area of his life things were going just the way he wanted — at least, this was almost true. He was worried about his daughter, but she would whip into line. Lillian, a woman in town, was holding back, but in time he would have her. He was picking up two more parcels of land. The deals had not been completed, but they would be. Here and there, along the way, a man ran into a few difficulties, but if you held to your goal there was nothing to worry about.

His wife had just died. He would not have admitted it to anyone but he was rather glad that she was gone. For years she had never bothered him, she had been a quiet, respectful, submissive person, but even her presence, sometimes, was a deterrent to what he wanted. It was a relief not to have to think about her any more. And it was going to be a pleasure, thinking about who might take her place someday. Not Lillian. She was a woman of the moment and as fine as she was, she didn't have the personality he wanted in a new wife. In the days ahead he would become an important man in the Territory. His wife should be a match to him.

It was late afternoon. He was in his office at the ranch. This, actually, was where he transacted most of his business. His records were here. He did have a place in town, and he called it an office, but it was important only on occasion.

There was a knock on the door. Justine looked that way. He guessed who was there and he said, "Come on in, George."

George Adsell stepped inside. He was Justine's foreman, but he was much more than that. To an extent he was an associate. He thought the way Justine did. He was as tall and heavy as Justine, and he wore a mustache but no beard. Under forty years old, a younger Justine, he was an aggressive man, but he was careful with his boss. He was a perfect ally. He never went too far.

He was not a talkative man. He came right to the point. He said, "Rossiter's here." Then he stood waiting.

"At the ranch?" Justine asked.

"No. He's in town. Took a room in the hotel. Want to see him?"

"Do I have to?"

"Nope. I talked to him. He wants his money."

"Half the money."

"That's what I meant. Five hundred dollars. He gets the rest after."

"Can you trust him?"

"I figure so. He won't talk about who hired him. He makes his living this way. He's a killer."

"Do you think he can gun down Gallard?"

"He figures he can. He met Gallard once, knows about him. He's not afraid of him."

Justine looked toward the window. "How fast will Rossiter move? How will he manage it?"

"I don't know how he'll operate," George said. "That's his problem. It might take a day or two, not more than that. Rossiter won't go after him. He'll plan to gun him down in town so it'll look like a fair fight. Afterwards, Rossiter will ride out. I'll have to meet him somewhere, and pay him the extra five hundred."

Justine was silent for a moment, then he opened his desk drawer and took out a money box. He unlocked it, took out a pouch. It was fairly heavy. He held it out to George, and said, "Here you are, gold, a thousand dollars. I hope we're not makin' a mistake."

"You want to get rid of Gallard, don't you?" George said.

"Sure I do. He could stir up the whole valley."

"So now he won't," George said. "He'll get himself killed in a gunfight that you had nothing to do with. Nothin' could be better than that."

"Just get it done," Justine said. "What about Frank Thompson and Ed Broadwell? Have you found them?"

"Nope. Not yet. Ain't seen 'em anywhere. They're not in town, that's for sure. And they didn't leave by stagecoach. Could be they rode out themselves."

"Where would they have gone?"

"Can't figure."

"They got to be around somewhere," Justine said. "We'll give 'em another day to show up. Where's my daughter?"

"Kathy?" George shrugged. "She's out ridin', somewhere, alone. When she wants to ride alone, that's what she does. She doesn't pay any attention to me."

"Me either," Justine said. "I wish she was back at school."

"When does she leave?"

"Next month — unless she decides to stay here."

George blinked, and he sounded interested. "You mean she might stay here?"

"How do I know what she'll do? I wish she'd been a boy."

"She's a nice girl," George said.

He moistened his lips. The expression that touched his face would have been hard to read. He started to speak again but held back, and was silent.

"You better get to town," Justine said. "Give Rossiter half his money an' get things started."

"Sure. I'm on my way," George said. And he turned and headed for the door.

Justine watched the man leave. He was scowling; he felt strangely tense and on edge, and mildly excited. He would feel that way for several days — until Rossiter had finished his job and left the country. He didn't much like to do this, but it was something that had to be done. Tom Gallard, to an extent, was the leader of the small, independent ranchers. Most of them would listen to him. They might even follow him in an attempt to hang on to their property. If something happened to him, some other person might take his place, but it was hard to see who it might be. He could think of no one who could take Gallard's place.

He got up, walked to the window, looked out in the yard. George Adsell had mounted his horse and started for the gate. And someone was riding in. It was Kathy.

"Good," Justine said under his breath, and he relaxed for a moment.

Kathy rode on into the yard. She had to ride past George, and she did. He had stopped to say something to her and she answered him, over her shoulder. Even from a distance Justine could see the way George was frowning.

"Good for her," Justine said.

He had not heard what had been said but he could see that Kathy had not stopped. He knew why. Kathy didn't like George. She never had. He had explained to her once that George was important to him, and Kathy had said, "All right, you be nice to him, but don't tell me what to do. I pick my own friends."

He approved that attitude. In fact, he rather liked all the tendencies about her that worried him, her recklessness, her stubbornness, her independence. She was small, slender, blond, blue-eyed, beautiful, and almost twenty years old, and she had her own ideas about what was right and what was wrong. Most of the time she thought he was wrong. Sometimes they had real arguments.

But he didn't mind that. He had never listened to a woman, he never would.

He turned away to stand in front of a map that was nailed to the wall. It was a map of the valley. His valley. A third of it belonged to him already. He had spent five years settling in and consolidating his position. Now he was ready to move on, take on more land, maybe another third. He marked just what he wanted this year. It included the Gallard ranch.

The next day was Saturday. Tom Gallard and Myrt sometimes went to town on Saturday. On rare occasions, Red went with them. Lately they had been avoiding the town on Saturday, and they did this time. They might ride in some day next week.

Gallard seemed a little restless that afternoon. He said, several times, that maybe they should have risked a trip to town, just to see what people had to say.

"Nonsense," Myrt said. "If anything important has happened, we'll hear about it."

"I don't like to feel afraid to go to town," Gallard muttered.

"Could we take a trip tomorrow?" Myrt asked. "We might go and visit the Oldrings. I'd like to see Sally. And of course Carl and Fran."

"Hmmm. We ought to be able to do that," Gallard said, and he turned to Red. "How about you? Like to go with us?"

"I can find work here," Red answered.

"He's afraid of Fran Oldring," Myrt said, but she smiled.

"I'm not afraid of any girl," Red said.

"She's a nice person," Gallard said. "And so is her father. I'd like to talk to him about Justine and about what might happen. Let's ride out there tomorrow."

"Me, too?" Red asked.

"Yes, you too," Gallard said. "You can stand it."

They left for the Oldring ranch the next morning. Myrt had made up three food packages to be carried with them; that gave them one package apiece. In Red's package were several paper-wrapped glass jars of jelly, and there was one jar of pickles. Gallard's package had the meat, and the vegetables were in Myrt's. This was customary with the Gallards. If they went anywhere involving a meal, they took along food. Red had learned that long ago. "The Gallards," Myrt said, "always pay their way."

Red was not looking forward to the day. Myrt would enjoy talking to Sally Oldring, and Gallard and Carl Oldring would have a lot to say to each other. That left him to Fran, and she would probably be as uncomfortable as he would. She was a nice girl, he supposed, growing up just like he was, but what could he talk to her about? He was part Indian, of course, and at some places that would have made a difference, but not at the Oldrings. They had never seemed to understand that he was different. He remembered that about them, and felt better. He wished there could have been more people in the valley like the Oldrings.

They rode horseback because a wagon would have been too slow. Myrt could ride a horse almost as well as a man. She was amazing in a good many ways. She had never been confined to the kitchen. He had learned that before she married Gallard she had been a teacher. That might have explained why he had learned to read and write so quickly. He had a good teacher. She had been a mother, too, and she still spoke warmly of her son, Andy. He had hurt her, terribly. She said that herself, yet if he walked in tomorrow she would have thrown herself in his arms. He had done wrong. She knew that but she had forgiven him. Gallard, himself, seldom spoke about Andy, but Red had the feeling that he was looking forward to seeing him some day, after he got out of prison.

It looked like this might be a nice day. The weather was clear; there was hardly any wind. They made it to Seven Mile gulch in good time and the Oldrings seemed glad they had come.

It was a nice day for the Gallards and the Oldrings. It was even a good day for Red. No one pushed him at Fran Oldring. He was mostly left alone. He listened to some of what Gallard and Oldring had to say about the possibilities of trouble in the valley, and he was interested in Oldring's attitude. "Justine's got to be stopped," the man said. "We ought to have a meeting, get the other ranchers together. You're the man to call the meeting."

"Why me?" Gallard said.

"Folks will listen to you," Oldring said.

"I don't want to start trouble."

"I don't either, but what are we going to do? Get gobbled up? I think we ought to get together — plan something."

"I'll have to think about it," Gallard said.

They had dinner in the middle of the afternoon and a little later and after the dishes had been done, Red was pushed at Fran, but in a way he didn't mind. Oldring said, "Red, you like horses, don't you?"

"More than anything else," Red answered.

"Then I want you to take a look at Fran's new horse. We bought him from two mustangers and he hasn't been gentled. He might even be an outlaw. I'm not sure about him."

Fran spoke up. "He can be gentled."

Red looked at her. She was tall and thin, even bony, and her long, black hair was in braids. Her face was rather plain but she was quite tanned and she had dark, steady eyes. She looked rather nice when she smiled or when she was excited, like now. She was about his own age.

"Has anyone tried to ride him?" Red asked.

The girl shook her head. "Not yet."

"Could I try him?"

"Why? He's my horse."

"We were going to bring in a wrangler," Oldring said. "You know that, Fran. Why don't we see what Red can do. They tell me he's good with horses."

"But why can't I gentle my own horse?"

Oldring shook his head. "I love you too much."

Fran bit her lips, then she looked at Red, critically, and she said, finally, "Do you want to see him?"

"Yes." Red nodded. "I'd like to."

"If you beat him . . ."

"I won't beat him."

"Then come on."

They walked to the old corral. The new horse was penned there, alone. He saw them coming and he danced to the far side of the enclosure, and stood watching them, tense and nervous. Fran said his name was Night.

The two older men talked about the black horse and his good points. The two women just watched. Fran looked at Red narrowly and she seemed worried. Red had nodded, but his eyes had brightened. He thought: "Here is a real horse — the kind I have always wanted." He could not be sure, but he thought he was right about the horse.

"Wait here," he said abruptly. "Keep talking. Don't pay any attention to me."

He moved part way around the corral fence, stopped for a moment then moved on and stopped again. The horse was watching him closely. He seemed to have forgotten the others. He threw his head from side to side, snorted, reared up into the air and pounded down with his forefeet.

"Easy there, Night," Red said quietly. "Easy. Easy. You know, you've got to get used to me."

He climbed to the top rail of the corral and sat there for a time, talking to the horse. Just talking, quietly, pleasantly.

The horse watched him. He reared up into the air, pounded his forefeet to the earth. Red could see the twitching of the horse's skin, but that wasn't a sign of fear. It was a sign of excitement. The horse's head was high, the short ears were pointed forward.

Red slid down inside the corral. He stood there for a moment, then he stepped forward. He took another step forward, and another, and another. He kept talking in a monotone.

The words he used were not important. He could have said anything. It was his voice that counted, the sound of it. And maybe it was important that he didn't hurry, that he was slow in everything that he did. He knew there were a great many things he didn't know about horses but he had learned he had an instinctive way of handling them. He always talked to them just as though they were people. And of course he loved them. Maybe that counted. Maybe a horse could sense how he felt.

He took two more steps toward the horse, and stopped. He was still talking. The horse reared up into the air, snorted, pounded down at the earth, and then, with no warning, charged straight at him.

Red stood where he was. He could have been run down but that didn't happen. Instead, the horse pulled up in front of him, reared his forefeet high into the air and slammed them down, just inches from where Red was standing. The horse snorted again, wheeled away. He circled the corral several times, then stopped and faced him, but from a distance.

"That's all right," Red said. "Take your time, Night. There's no rush about this. We've got all afternoon to get to know each other."

He took a step toward the horse, another and another. The horse snorted and backed away. It took twenty more minutes to reach the horse and stretch out his hand and touch him, but he finally did that.

"Be seeing you again, Night," he said, still in the same quiet voice. "Yep, I'll sure be seeing you again." He smiled and turned away, started back across the corral.

He was halfway across the corral when Oldring shouted a warning and Red heard the horse pounding toward him, but all Night did was to circle him then pound back to the far side of the corral. There, he snorted defiantly.

Red continued to the corral fence. He climbed over it, nodded to Oldring, and he said to Fran, "That's quite a horse you've got there. He's no outlaw."

"When could you ride him?" Oldring asked.

"Next time I see him, maybe. Or the time after."

"When he charged you . . ."

"He was just talking back," Red said. "I don't blame him."

Oldring turned to Gallard. "Can Red find the time to finish the job here?"

"It's all right with me," Gallard said.

"I'll try to stop by tomorrow afternoon," Red said, "or I'll make it the next afternoon. I don't want Night to forget me."

It was dark before they left for home and it was amazing to Red how much he had enjoyed himself. He blamed this chiefly on the horse. He was quite an animal, high spirited, exciting. He might have to make several trips to Seven Mile Gulch before he was through with the horse. Fran would be there every time, but she didn't seem to be much of a problem.

They didn't talk much on the way home, everyone seemed tired. They turned in early.

Two men came by Monday morning, Fred Kreel and Mike Ingerhall. Kreel lived south of the Gallard place, Ingerhall, farther down the valley. Red and Gallard had been working on the roof of the barn but when the two men rode in, Gallard climbed down to talk to them. Red stayed on the roof. He went on working.

Kreel and Ingerhall did not stay very long. They rode away together, and strangely, they didn't stop at the house to say hello to Myrt before they left. Normally, they would have done that.

Red had expected Gallard to climb back on the roof and go on working, but he didn't. Instead, after the two men left, he walked down to the river. He stayed there for a time then walked back, and he was nodding to himself, as though he had made some decision. When he got closer to the barn he called, "Red, I want you to come down here."

"Right away," Red said. But he was thinking: "Something's happened. Maybe the trouble is starting."

While he was coming down from the roof Myrt showed up in the doorway to the house. She called, "Wasn't that Fred Kreel and Mike Ingerhall? Where did they go?"

"I guess they had to hurry home," Gallard said. "Can you fix up two sandwiches for me and Red? We've got

45

to take a trip up the river. We won't get back until after noon."

"I thought we were going to stay home," Myrt said.

"We did plan to stay here," Gallard said. "But I hear they're putting a dam across the river and I want to see why."

"I thought we had trouble with water already."

"I don't think this will hurt us," Gallard said. "But I want to be sure."

"Give me ten minutes to put up the lunch," Myrt said, and she went back inside the house.

Gallard turned to Red. "Mind saddling up two of the horses? I want to go to the house for a minute."

"I'll get the horses," Red said.

He turned away and he thought he had been wrong about the nearness of trouble. He and Gallard would be heading up the river, to see a dam.

He got his saddle and Gallard's, then he picked out two horses, caught them and saddled them. He put on his gun belt. He had not been wearing it while he had been on the roof of the barn, but when a man rode out anywhere it was proper to wear it. He checked it, made sure it was loaded, then slid it into its holster.

Gallard came out of the house carrying the sandwiches, and hurried to the horses.

Myrt had followed him. She called, "Hey, wait a minute."

Gallard waited for her. He was hugged and kissed, and he laughed and said, "Many thanks, Myrt. You're quite a girl."

46

"And you're quite a man," Myrt said. "Hurry home, always."

Gallard moved on to where Red was standing with the horses. He put the sandwiches in one of the saddlebags, took the reins of his horse, and mounted. He waved to Myrt, then led the way to the river. Red mounted his horse and followed him.

They headed upriver and for a time Gallard was silent. He frowned a bit; he might have been thinking. After awhile he did have several things to say but he didn't mention exactly where they were going, or why. Red asked no questions. He was curious but he knew that eventually he would find out what this was about.

When they came to the point where Squaw Creek cut into the river they broke away, headed up the creek. This was not the right way. If they kept on in this direction they might reach town.

In about four more miles Gallard reined up, and looked at Red. "It's only about eleven o'clock. Do you think you could eat this early?"

"I told you once that I was always hungry," Red said. "That's still true."

"Good. Then we'll eat," Gallard said.

They dismounted, tied their horses and found a place to sit in the shade. It was pleasantly warm. Red had brought their canteens. Gallard got the sandwiches. There were four of them, meat sandwiches. Myrt had added two pieces of cake. This was a good lunch.

They said very little while they ate. Red would have been silent, anyhow, but that was not normal for Gallard. He usually had something to say. Finally, he did. He said, "Red, we're not headed in the right direction. Maybe you noticed."

"I noticed," Red said.

"We're on our way to town," Gallard said. "I didn't want to tell Myrt where we were going, because she would worry. I don't want to go there myself and I don't think you ought to go, but now and then you've got to take a chance. Ben Justine is going to be in town, today. I learned that from Kreel and Ingerhall. He's going to be at the bank, at noon, and I want to see him."

Red nodded, but he was silent. He waited for Gallard to go on.

The man did. He looked away, frowning, and he said, "Justine comes to town quite often. I could have seen him almost any time, but I didn't. I don't care for him. I've left him alone. I'd like to leave him alone, now, but I guess I can't. Mike Ingerhall says that if there's anyone who can talk to Ben Justine, it's me. Kreel said the same thing. Both of them think that if I put it on the line, Justine might listen. I doubt if he will, but someone should talk to him. Someone should tell him what might happen if the whole valley blows up."

"He won't listen," Red said.

"That's what I'm afraid of, but I've got to try." Gallard spoke slowly. "I've been waiting to see what Justine would do. This is wrong. I know what he's going to do. He's leaning that way already. I think he will go ahead but I ought to give him one chance to back off. I'm not going to beg and I'm not going to threaten. I

48

just want to tell him what might happen if he goes ahead."

"He won't like it," Red said. "If he's got any of his men around they might try to gun you down."

"No, I don't think so," Gallard said. "It wouldn't look good to the people if his men went after me. I think Justine wishes I wasn't here, but I am. If he could get rid of me . . ."

"What do you want me to do?" Red asked.

"I didn't want to go alone," Gallard said. "Besides, it helps to have someone else, nearby. If a single man went after me, that would be that. I'd take my chance. But if there were two men, or if there were several, they would have to take in consideration the fact that I was not alone. I just want you with me, that's about all."

Red straightened his shoulders. He took a deeper breath. Of course he had no notion about what might happen when they reached town. There was a good chance they would ride in and ride out, and that would be that. But if there was any trouble he would be there, to stand at Gallard's side. He had a place in the scheme of things. It was good to know where a man stood.

"I think we'll ride straight to the bank," Gallard said. "We'll dismount, tie our horses, and go in. If Justine is already there I'll talk to him, say what I have to, then we'll step outside, climb on our horses and leave. We might be there fifteen minutes. That's the way I hope things will work out. It's what I'm counting on. There's a chance, of course, that something else might happen. If it does, we'll face that problem when we have to."

Red nodded, but he was silent. He never had much to say, but he listened, always, to Tom Gallard. He had learned a great deal from him, or at least he thought he had. Gallard had a blunt, realistic way of looking at things. He stood straight. He never leaned to either side, the easy way or the hard. And he was methodical, taking things step by step.

He was saying, now, "Red, I hate to mention this but I suppose I ought to. Things could go wrong any time. If I ever get smashed I hope you'll look after Myrt until she gets on her feet. I want to count on that."

Red gulped. He looked away and nodded, but he knew he would never be able to take Gallard's place. Never.

Gallard looked at his watch. It was twenty-five minutes to twelve. If they rode on, fairly promptly, they ought to be able to reach town a little before noon. Kreel had said, definitely, that Justine would be at the bank at noon.

He stood up, brushed off his lap, took a brief look at his hand gun then put it back into his holster. He said, "Come on, Red. Time to get under way."

They cut out to the road and followed it, and Gallard, looking ahead, told himself: "I should have done this two weeks ago, or maybe earlier than that. I should have gone to Justine and reminded him what would happen if he kept pushing down the valley. It might be too late to stop him now — or maybe I never could have — but I've got to try."

He slowed down, and explained to Red, in detail, why he was doing this, why it was important no matter what the result was. He was not defending himself, not justifying himself. He wanted Red to see the lesson in a situation like this. In the past two years he had spent a lot of time talking to Red about what he thought of as problems of living, of getting along together. Myrt had been the teacher, more than he, but he had tried to add a few practical suggestions.

"Thinking about Justine," he said gruffly, "you don't have to like him. You can even hate him if you give him a fair shake, if you can admit to yourself that he's got the right to have his own opinions even if they're not like yours. We're all on the same level, the good and the bad and the in-between. You ought to keep that in mind, always."

Red scowled, but after a moment he nodded.

It occurred to Gallard that there were dozens of things he still wanted to explain to Red, who could absorb only a certain amount. He didn't want to keep preaching too much. And maybe, some of the things he had wanted to say, were unnecessary. Red had grown to man-size. He had been able to avoid serious trouble, and in view of his background and of his Indian heritage, that was amazing. He could handle a rifle and a handgun, he could use his fists — and he knew something about avoiding trouble. Give him a chance and Red might do all right. Gallard was sure he had not made a mistake in giving him a home.

The town was just ahead. Gallard slowed down, Red kept beside him, and when Gallard checked his hand gun he noticed that Red was doing the same thing.

He scowled, and said, "Red, don't think about your gun. We're going to ride in, and ride out. That's all."

Red nodded. "Sure. I know."

Gallard looked ahead at the town. He felt tense and uneasy and he told himself it was foolish to feel this way. They were on the edge of a valleywide conflict if he couldn't talk to Justine, he knew that. It could break out at almost any moment, even today, but he hoped the fight could be put off, or even forgotten. If Justine would only listen . . .

CHAPTER
FOUR

Red was breathing a little faster, and his heart was pounding harder. He thought he was more alert than ever before. He was excited but he didn't think this showed in his face even though his lips had tightened. They were at the edge of town. Very soon they would reach the bank, the heart of the business area. Most likely they would ride in, spend a few minutes in the bank then move out, climb their horses and head home and nothing would happen. But something might. They could run into trouble, and if that happened he would be right there.

He had recalled, many times, the day when the Apaches had attacked his father's cabin. He had been frightened that day, but he had been able to crouch at his father's side, reload his guns. He had been able to help. This might be another instance like that, but he was no longer a boy. He could do more than load a rifle.

They had moved past the first houses. Not far ahead were the first stores and the livery stable was across the street. A few people were in sight, moving along the board walks, or here and there clustered in groups. A number of saddle horses were tied at the rails; there were several teams and wagons.

"A fair crowd," Gallard said. "Not too many people around. I'm glad of that, less chance of trouble. Looks like there's plenty of room to tie our horses in front of the bank."

Red nodded, but he said nothing.

They were passing the Valley Feed Store. A woman came out, noticed them and waved. Red knew her. She was Mrs. Adams. Her husband owned the store but he had been ill for months. Mrs. Adams had taken his place. She was still young and attractive. She had always been nice to him.

Since she had waved, he waved back. And Gallard touched his hat.

"Can you stop in for a minute, Tom?" the woman called.

"Not right now," Gallard said. "We might be able to stop on the way back, Lillian."

"Do that if you can. How's Myrt?"

"Fine as ever."

"Bring her to town next time."

"Might do that," Gallard said.

They had slowed down, nearly stopped, but now Gallard shook the reins, loosened them, and his horse moved on. Red followed him.

They passed the saloon. There might have been a dozen men on the porch and in front of the doors. Red took a quick look that way. He noticed a group of four men standing together and looking at him, or maybe Gallard. They were four of Justin's riders and they seem to have tensed. Red thought: "Something's going to happen. We rode in all right, but when it comes to riding out . . ."

"Here we are," Gallard said, and he turned his horse in toward the hitching rail.

Red swung that way with him. He dismounted, tied his horse loosely the way Gallard had shown him, then joined Gallard in front of the bank. They went in together, closed the door behind them.

There was a small lobby. Directly ahead was a counter, a part of it grilled off. There were two customers. One was talking to the banker, who was across the counter. The other customer was at the grilled window. Red didn't know either one, and Justine was not here unless he was in the private office, to the rear.

Gallard raised his voice. "Sorry to bother you, Charlie, but are you expecting Ben Justine?"

"I was," the banker answered. "He was supposed to be here by noon but George Adsell came in a few minutes ago to report that Justine couldn't make it. I'll be free in a moment. Anything I can do for you?"

"Don't think so," Gallard said, frowning. "I wanted to see Ben."

"He might be in later. Why don't you ask George Adsell? He's somewhere down the street."

"I might do that," Gallard said.

He stood there, halfway to the counter, hesitating, possibly thinking about what to do. Red stepped back and to the side. He looked through the window and back toward the saloon. He could see several men on the far side of the street but he noticed no one in particular. At least he saw no more of Justine's riders.

Gallard swung around, joined him. "I suppose we might as well leave. I might be able to see Justine if we waited but it might not be wise to do that. I wonder . . ."

He broke off, was silent. Red glanced at him. He was staring through the window, toward a man who was standing near the corner of a building. Red peered at the man Gallard was watching. He was not much to look at, a small man, made to seem smaller by the way he hunched. He wore a black hat, coat and trousers. His gun was holstered low. That was the way Gallard wore his gun. It was the way Red wore his. The brim of the man's hat shadowed his face but Red would have guessed the man was middle aged, or older.

Gallard said thoughtfully, "If I'm right that's Jules Rossiter, a gunfighter I met in Tucson a good many years ago. Don't know what he's doing here. Maybe it's an accident, or maybe . . ."

"Justine could have hired him," Red said.

"I sure hope not," Gallard said. "Anyhow, he's not looking this way. What do you say we ride out of here, while we can?"

"Is he that bad?"

"Worse. Let's move."

He headed for the door. Red took another quick look through the window. Rossiter, if that was his name, had turned his head to look down the street. And he lifted his hand to cover his mouth, possibly to cover a cough.

"Come on, Red," Gallard said from the door.

56

Red joined him. They stepped outside but even as they did the man across the street swung to look their way, then moved across the board walk and stepped into the street.

"He's coming this way," Red said.

"Yes, he's coming this way," Gallard said. "And I was right about who it is — Jules Rossiter. I can make another guess. I'm the reason he's here. Red, I want you to get on your horse and ride out of here. I'll join you if I can."

Red didn't say a word. He didn't say he would ride out, or that he wouldn't. They were on the walk in front of the bank. Red took a quick look toward the saloon. There were more people on the street, quite a few more, and most were looking this way. It seemed almost as though they were anticipating something.

Rossiter had taken several steps in their direction, he was nearly in the middle of the street. He stopped suddenly, raised his voice. "Gallard! Gallard, you remember me!"

"Yes, I remember you."

"Come out on the street. Want to talk to you for a minute."

Gallard hesitated, but he spoke to Red. "No way out of it, I guess. I'll see what he wants. You climb your horse, head for home, right away."

Red still didn't say anything. He watched as Gallard stepped down from the walk, moved between two of the horses and out into the street to face Rossiter.

"Should have done this a long time ago," Rossiter said. "I owe you from way back in Tucson, remember?"

"I remember," Gallard said.

"Then you know what I'm going to do," Rossiter said. "Reach for your gun, any time."

"No sense in that," Gallard said. "What would I want to do that for?"

"You might as well try. I'm gonna kill you anyhow. I promised to do it a long time ago."

Gallard started to speak. "I don't see why we don't . . ."

"Too much gab," Rossiter said, interrupting. His voice had sharpened, his body had dropped into a lower crouch. "Reach for your gun, Gallard. *Reach for it now!*"

Red was staring at Rossiter, watching him. His right hand was at the end of a bowed arm, the fingers extended like claws. They slapped in at his holster then whipped up, lifting his gun, centering it. He fired it. There was an echoing shot. It was Gallard who was responsible for that but his shot must have been wide.

Rossiter stood there in the street. He fired again at the stumbling figure of Tom Gallard. He fired a third time as Gallard sprawled to the ground. For an instant, then, he stood there, peering at the man he had shot. Right after that he started reloading his gun. There was a tight, ugly smile on his face. He seemed to be nodding to himself.

Red saw what had happened, saw all that had happened. He was numb at the suddenness of the gun duel, not really believing it yet. Hardly anything had been said. Gallard had started a mild objection but before he could finish Rossiter had cut in, and stopped the talking. He had not wanted any talking. It would seem that he had come here for one, specific reason — to kill Gallard. He had succeeded. Gallard was dead! Dead — as suddenly as that — in the space of a few moments.

Red wiped a hand across his face. It seemed he had stopped thinking. He tried to get his mind working. Gallard had told him to leave but how could he do that? What he ought to do was — what? He didn't know.

He realized, abruptly, that he had moved out into the street, and that a crowd had gathered. He was close to where Gallard was lying. He knelt down, took a brief look at the man in the street, but knew there was nothing he could do. Gallard was dead.

He stood up, looked around. The crowd he had noticed was still here, and among them, watching, was Jules Rossiter. There were a good many in the crowd he must have known but he could see no one but Rossiter. Rossiter, the outlaw, the killer who sold his gun for hire. How much had he been paid for the death of Tom Gallard? Who had put up the money?

The man had started to turn away but Red shouted, "Wait a minute, Rossiter. Where do you think you're going?"

The man stopped, looked back, and those who were standing near him moved away, out of the danger of a stray shot.

"Any time," Red said. His voice was high, grating. "Grab your gun again — see if you're lucky."

"Don't try it, kid," Rossiter said. "Didn't you see what I did to Gallard?"

"That's why I'm here," Red said. "I came with him. He asked me to take his place."

Rossiter hesitated but then he nodded. "Another damned fool," he said flatly.

His gun was out, but there had been another shot, an earlier shot. It had come from Red's gun. It smashed through Rossiter's chest and Rossiter's shot went wide. He reeled backwards, sat down, rolled over on his side. There was a bloody froth on his lips.

Red stood quietly where he was. No one spoke. The crowd seemed stunned. Red looked from side to side, and tried to keep his face from showing anything. He was suddenly uneasy, not sure what he ought to do. He was wondering what would happen now. He told himself: "I have killed a man. He was a hired killer, his death was fair, but there are some men who are going to say that Rossiter was a white man and I am a breed — an Indian. So what should I do?" Another thought crossed his mind. "Gallard said I was to take care of Myrt. First, I think, she would have wanted me to take care of Gallard's body — take him home."

He took a steadying breath, looked from side to side, then he spoke. "I want a team and wagon. Who can lend me a team and wagon? I want to take Tom Gallard home."

A man stepped out into the street. It was Bernie Meyers, the owner of the general store. He said, "I've got a team and wagon you can use. I'll go get them."

"Thanks," Red said.

Then he stood waiting, and the waiting was hard. He had put his hand gun back into its holster. He touched it lightly, just to be sure it was there, and he tried not to look at anyone. A minute passed, and another, and another. Some of the crowd had left but a good many men were still on the street To one side were some of the Justine riders, grouped together, talking. Another group, valley riders, were having their own conference. Dry Fork had a sheriff, Dave Tanner, but he didn't seem to be around. It could be that he was purposely not here — so he could not interfere between Rossiter and Gallard. Dave Tanner was Justine's good friend.

Some men gathered around Rossiter, carried his body away. There was more talk along the street. Beef Causey had joined the Justine crowd. He belonged there, was one of them, but Red had not noticed him before. He was a giant of a man, big, heavy, a bruiser. He had killed a man in a fight about two months ago by breaking his back. Gallard had said that he was a man to avoid, but in a way, most of the Justine crowd was dangerous.

A team and wagon came down the street. Bernie Meyers was driving it. He reined up near Gallard's body, summoned three other men to help him, climbed down and took part in lifting Gallard's body into the wagon. He had remembered a blanket.

After that the storekeeper turned to Red. "Want me to drive home with you? My wife can look after the store."

Red shook his head. "Thanks, but I can manage alone. I'll return your team and wagon."

"I'll pick it up myself," the storekeeper said. "Tell Myrt I'll be down to see her. Tell her how sorry I am about — about what happened."

Red touched his gun, made sure it was well holstered. He tied his horse and Gallard's to the back of the wagon, then climbed to the seat, reached for the reins, and started the team. He ignored the Justine riders, he ignored everyone else, headed down the street. From the edge of town he would swing east, toward the Gallard ranch.

It was a long ride home. It was one he would never forget. The sun burned down from the sky. There was scarcely any wind. The team kept moving but he had to touch them occasionally with the whip and remind them that they were supposed not to stop.

His mind had been active for a time but then it seemed to go to sleep. He woke it up, did more thinking, but he was not sure that this was helping him, that it was getting him anywhere. What was he going to say to Myrt when he drove in? How could he explain what had happened? He couldn't think of any words that wouldn't be hurtful. He wished, now, that he had brought the storekeeper with him. Bernie might have known what to say.

Another problem hammered at him. Gallard had asked him to help Myrt if anything happened to him, but how was he going to be able to do that? He could try to stand by her but what would happen if some of Justine's men rode in? Up to today he had stayed in the background, he had been careful to avoid any trouble.

As an instance, he had never entered either of Dry Fork's two saloons, aware that if he had done so he might have been trapped into a fight. He had sidestepped any issues — up to today. But today . . .

He looked back at what had happened to him today, and he wondered if Rossiter's death hadn't been partly accidental. He was good with his gun. He knew that. He had been practicing for almost four years. But Rossiter was a professional. He might have made one mistake, he might not have tried hard enough. In any case, Red didn't want to think of himself as better than Rossiter. He still meant to go on, practicing. But what would they be saying in town — that he had turned gunhand? Some might say that, and some of Justine's men might have decided they wanted to test him.

It had been a long way home but suddenly it wasn't. Home was just ahead. He came over the last rise and there was the house and the clustering ranch buildings. He knew that someone might have ridden here, faster, across country, and might have told Myrt what had happened, but it was more likely no one had been here. He could see no saddled horses at the corral.

The wagon moved on down the road. Red had no idea of what he was going to say when Myrt showed up. He had not been able to think up the right words. He drove into the yard, checked the team, and sat in the seat of the wagon, sweating.

The door opened. Myrt appeared. She stepped outside, stopped, and said, "That's not our wagon, not our team."

"The team and wagon belong to Bernie Meyers," Red answered. "I borrowed them. I — we went to town."

She seemed to sense what was coming and he could see her brace herself. She asked, "Where's Tom? Has something happened?"

He nodded. He couldn't seem to speak.

"Has he been hurt?" Her voice choked up. "Is he — do you mean . . ."

"I brought him home," Red said.

He didn't look at her when he said that. He stared straight ahead. He thought: "She'll scream. Or worse then that, she'll faint, and then what will I do? I never should have come home alone."

There was no screaming. There were no sounds at all. He looked toward her. She had backed to the wall of the house and was leaning there, both hands spread out, bracing herself. Even from where he was sitting he could see the pallor of her face. She was breathing heavily.

She spoke suddenly, her voice coming in jerks. "You'll have to — drive the wagon — closer — to the door. We'll have to — to carry him inside. He's — he's quite heavy."

The sun went down. It started growing dark. A cooling breeze came up and it was welcomed. Red sat on a wood box near the barn. Bernie's team had been cared for, then stalled in the barn; the wagon had been moved off to the side of the yard. There had been no visitors but there had not been much time. They would have visitors tomorrow — or maybe tonight. Gallard's body had been carried inside, placed on the bed. Myrt, most likely, was with him, crying. But she had not cried while they carried him inside. She had not cried while he had been there.

He was still wearing his hand gun. His rifle was nearby. As long as it had been light he had kept watch, looking up the valley road. He thought that surely Justine and his men wouldn't bother them at a time like this, but he was not sure about that. He was afraid he was not sure about anything.

As it turned dark, lamplight showed through the kitchen window. A moment later Myrt appeared in the doorway. She called, "Red! Red, where are you?"

"Out here, Myrt," he answered.

"Come on in. You don't nave to sit in the dark. Besides, it's time for supper."

He walked forward. "I can get something for myself. You don't have to . . ."

"Supper's almost ready," Myrt said.

He washed outside, entered the house. The stove had been fired, the smell of food was in the air. Two places had been set at the table, one for him, one for Myrt.

She motioned to the table. "Sit down, Red. Nothing on the stove will burn. Before we eat I want you to tell me all that happened."

Red sat down. He told her what had happened in town, how Gallard had been killed, then what he had done. This took only a few minutes.

Myrt seemed to listen intently. She asked hardly any questions. She did say she had heard of Rossiter and she said, "Red, you shouldn't have done what you did, but in a way, I'm glad. If Tom had to die, I don't think it would have been right for Jules Rossiter to go on living."

Red frowned. "Tom said that Rossiter would never have come here if someone hadn't sent for him."

"Justine?"

"Yes. He's the one who ought to be killed."

"That will happen, probably. But it's not up to you, Red. You can't go around the country killing people."

"Rossiter did."

"But look what happened to him. Let me tell you something that Tom told me. It's an important thing to know. No matter how fast a man is, sooner or later he runs across a man who is faster. If you start your life with a gun, that's the way you will end it. I want you to remember that. I want you to live, Red."

Red nodded, but he was afraid he would not live very long if he stayed around here. Justine had too many men and too many were good with their guns. He could never challenge them all.

"We will have the funeral day after tomorrow," Myrt said. "Some of our friends will want to come. That gives them enough time. Now, we will eat."

It was a good meal. Red was able to eat rather well but he noticed that Myrt ate hardly anything. He was just finishing when he heard the sounds of horses drumming into the yard.

He got quickly to his feet, and he reached to touch his holstered gun, made sure it drew easily. It occurred to him he had made two mistakes in town, facing

Rossiter. He could not remember that he had checked that his gun was loose in its holster. And he had been burning with anger when he faced Rossiter. Gallard had said that a man, riding his anger, was a fool. He had made two mistakes in Dry Fork. He could never risk that again.

"You can go to the door," Myrt said. "I'll clear the table."

He took a sharp breath. "What if it's Justine?"

She shook her head. "It won't be."

He moved toward the door, opened it a crack, but he didn't show himself. He called out, "Who's there?"

The answer was blunt "It's Dave Tanner."

Red looked around at Myrt, who nodded, and walked toward him. She reached the door, opened it wider, and she called out, "What is it, Sheriff?"

"I'd like a word with Red Pardee, Mrs. Gallard." The man's voice was gruff. "Hate to bother you at a time like this, but it can't be helped."

Myrt hesitated, but then she nodded. "Won't you come in, Mr. Tanner?"

"No. Just send the man out here," Tanner replied.

Myrt was frowning. She shook her head definitely. "I think it would be better if you come in here. Just you, Mr. Tanner. Not the men with you. The kitchen is rather small."

There was a momentary silence. Maybe there was a conference outside. Red didn't know. He was tense, worried. Why did the sheriff want him? He felt cornered. That wasn't a good way to feel.

Myrt looked around at him and she said, "Red, don't draw your gun. Keep your temper. Things are going to be much worse than this."

He backed away from the door, took a steadying breath, then straightened up and stood waiting.

Myrt looked outside again then she moved to the side. Footsteps approached the door and a moment later Dave Tanner showed up. He was a short man, round shouldered, and he was growing old. His face was deeply wrinkled and he had watery, grey eyes. White whiskers bristled in his chin and throat and when he pulled his hat off he showed that he was almost bald.

The man took a sharp look at Red, then he spoke to Myrt. "Like I said, I hate to bother you. Just came by to pick up Red Pardee. I've got to ride him to town."

"Why?" Myrt asked.

The man cleared his throat. "Maybe he didn't tell you what he did in town!"

"He told me what he did. He killed the man who shot my husband. Where were you when it happened, Mr. Tanner?"

"I was out of town. I'd been called away, but . . ."

"You knew Jules Rossiter was there, waiting for my husband, but you did nothing to prevent what happened. Why, Mr. Tanner?"

"Wasn't no call for it, ma'am."

"Wasn't there?" Myrt asked. "Jules was a known killer, a professional gunhawk. My husband was a rancher."

Definitely, Tanner was uncomfortable. He shifted his feet, cleared his throat again, then he said, "Ma'am, you just don't understand. Men who wear guns, use 'em. Ain't much I can do about it. But about Red Pardee . . ."

"Yes. What about Red?" Myrt said. "Why do you want him?"

"Some of the men think he pulled his gun too fast, didn't give Rossiter an even break."

"Well, Red?" Myrt asked.

"It was a fair fight," Red said. "Who said it wasn't?"

"Some of the men," Tanner said. "Got to take you in, anyhow. You'll get a hearing."

Myrt shook her head. "You haven't told me what men made the charge. Were they Justine's men?"

"Didn't ask," Tanner said.

"Well, who were they?"

Tanner showed a sudden flash of anger. "Now look here, Mrs. Gallard, you can't talk to me that way. I've got a job to do — an' that's all there is to it. Red Pardee, you come along with me."

Red shook his head. "No."

Tanner took a step toward him, but then he stopped. He glanced at Myrt, hesitated.

"I need him, here," Myrt said. "My husband has been killed. I have to arrange for the funeral, someone has to dig the grave. Would you expect me to do that?"

"Some of the men of the valley could . . ."

"I want Red to do that. Why don't you wait until after the funeral, before you arrest him — if that's what you mean to do."

"I ain't got the right to . . ."

"But that's what's going to happen," Myrt said. "Red's not going with you, tonight. You tell the men outside that I need Red until after the funeral — then, we'll see what happens. Good night, Mr. Tanner."

The sheriff motioned angrily with his arm. "Now look here, Mrs. Gallard . . ."

"Good night, Mr. Tanner," Myrt said.

"I told you . . ."

"Good night, Mr. Tanner."

The man hesitated. He moistened his lips and he took a look at Red, scowling. He looked again at Myrt. She was a tall, thin woman, pale and stern and standing very straight.

"You had better go," Red said quietly. "I will be here after the funeral."

"You'd better be," Tanner said. He stepped back to the door. "Don't you try to run out on me."

"Good night, Mr. Tanner," Myrt said again.

He glared at her, whirled around and headed for the door. He slammed it when he stepped outside.

CHAPTER
FIVE

Myrt stood tense, motionless, facing the door. But after Red could hear the sounds of the horses leaving, she turned around and she said, "Dave Tanner could have stopped the fight in town — or at least he could have tried. He didn't. I think I hate him."

"Hate him?" Red said. "I never heard you say anything like that before."

She bit her lips. "I try not to hate. I am trying, right now, not to hate Ben Justine, for I am sure that he is the one who sent for Jules Rossiter. I — I never expected anything like this. Red, I want you to go away."

"What!" He was startled.

"I want you to go away somewhere — to the mountains — or maybe you ought to go far, far away. To Chicago or to New York. No one there would know or care that you are partly Indian. I can give you enough money to get started."

Red shook his head. "What would I do with myself in Chicago or New York? What would I do anywhere else? I would feel lost."

"You'll get over it."

"But I wouldn't. And what about you, Myrt?"

"I'm a woman. Justine wouldn't dare to touch me."

"Then you don't know him."

"I don't think he would dare to touch me, but if you are worried about me I could move in with the Oldrings, for a time. Or I could stay with the Ingerhalls."

"And when they get smashed by Justine, what then?"

"That might not happen."

"But it will," Red said. "Tom thought Justine meant to take over the entire valley. Mr. Oldring thought so too."

"Yes, there might be trouble," Myrt said frowning. "But you are in more danger than I am. Justine never liked you because you are part Indian. Now he has more reason to hate you. You took Tom's place, you shot the man who killed him. You showed yourself as someone who might be dangerous. He's going to want to get rid of you. That's why he sent Dave Tanner to arrest you."

"You stopped that, Myrt."

"But I might not be able to do that again. That's why I want you to go away."

"No."

"But Red, you can't just stay here and — and wait for something to happen. I don't want to see you killed."

"I don't want that, either," Red admitted.

"Then that's the only thing you can do. Go away somewhere."

Red walked to the door. He opened it a crack and listened, but there was nothing to hear, so he closed it, and he said, "Myrt, how much time do you think I have?"

"To be safe, you ought to leave right now."

"What about tomorrow? Do you think it might be safe if I stayed here tomorrow?"

"It might be, but we can't be sure of it."

"What if I stayed here until after the funeral?"

"That would be the limit of your safety — and I don't know what might happen right after the funeral."

"I could have a fast horse nearby."

"You'll be taking a chance, Red. An unnecessary chance."

"Maybe not," Red said. "Justine's wife just died. He tried to get me arrested but I don't think he'll try anything until after the funeral."

"You would be safer if you left tonight. Tom kept a thousand dollars, put away here at home. It was for some sudden emergency. I'm going to give it to you."

"No. Keep it where it will be safe. Is it in gold?"

"Yes. Why?"

"Gold won't burn," Red answered. "I'm worried about the house."

"Not for tonight?"

"No, I don't think anything will happen until after the funeral, but after that, I don't know. I don't want you to stay here."

She nodded slowly. "I'll pick somewhere to stay. I — I wonder how much Justine is going to offer me, for the ranch?"

"You won't sell to him."

"Of course not. But I wonder what he'll offer — and I wonder what I'll say to him. I wish it was right for women to swear. I know all the words. I might even use some of them."

Her lips twisted, humorously, but then she turned and looked toward the bedroom door behind which her husband's body was lying. Her expression changed, tightened. Tears showed up in her eyes.

"I'll check things outside," Red said. "Be right back."

"Then you're not leaving tonight," Myrt said. "I'm glad. It'll be a comfort to know that you're here — but you really ought to leave."

"Later," Red said. "Maybe after the funeral."

He got the water pail, went outside to the well, got more water, filled the barrel in the kitchen. After that he checked the corral and the barn. The horses and chickens were quiet. The extra team in the barn made no extra sounds. There was a light wind from the north but it had not turned cold. The sky was clear. There seemed to be thousands of stars in the sky. Tom Gallard would have said that this was a gentle night, quiet and pleasant. They might have one more, but then what? He had to think about that.

Ben Justine sat at one of the tables in the Yucca saloon. He took another taste of his drink. This was his third, and the last one he would have tonight. He put a limit on his drinking. There were occasions when he might have more than three drinks but it took something special to make him go that far. Gallard was dead, had been gunned down — and that was all right, but the way Rossiter had been killed, right afterwards, put a sour end to what had happened.

George Adsell came in and sat down beside him. He reached for the bottle and one of the glasses on the table, and poured a drink. He looked tired and he was scowling. He was breathing the hard way that was almost typical of him.

"Any word on Tanner?" Justine asked.

"Not yet, but they ought to get back in the next half hour." George tossed off a drink. He poured another. "Don't worry about him. Tanner will do what you told him to."

"You don't know him like I do," Justine said. "You can trust Dave Tanner just about as far as you can spit in the wind."

"All right, if Tanner doesn't show up with the Injun we'll set up somethin' else."

"How good is Joe Stubbs with his gun?"

"Damned good. Faster than the Injun."

"Then how come Rossiter got killed?"

"He figgered the Injun was just a kid, not very good. He didn't do his best. Hell, it was just an accident that the Injun got him. He's fast, all right. But not like Joe Stubbs."

"I wish you'd fixed it some other way," Justine said. "Stubbs works for me."

"Sure, but Stubbs went with the posse tonight. He'll have a row with the Injun, ridin' in. That sets up the trouble tomorrow. The sheriff will let the Injun out of jail, give him his gun. Stubbs will be waitin' outside — an' he'll call him. That takes care of the Injun."

"Yeah — if things work out that way."

"If somethin' goes wrong, we'll try somethin' else," George said. "The big problem was Gallard, and Gallard is gone. There ain't no one left to round up the other ranchers. We're gonna go through this valley like a fire."

George took another drink, tossed it off. Then he leaned back, looked around the room.

"At least we saved half of Rossiter's fee," Justine said. "Where is it?"

"I'm gonna give it to Joe Stubbs — as a bonus," George said.

"Do you have to?"

"Why not? Ain't it worth it?" George was staring at the bar. He changed his voice, lowered it. "There she is — the girl I told you about — Rossiter's girl. At least, he spent a lot of time with her. Wonder if she talked. Maybe I better talk to her."

He poured a drink, gulped it, wiped his mouth then got to his feet.

"Nice looking girl," Justine said. "Where does Flo get 'em?"

"You better stick to Lillian," George said.

Justine's answer was sharp, hard. "Forget about Lillian. I told you that once before. I meant it."

"Sorry, Ben. Didn't mean to say it." He mumbled his words.

"Don't mention her again."

"Sure, boss. Don't you think I better talk to this girl that got to know Rossiter?"

"Do whatever you want to," Justine said. "I wish Tanner would get back with that Injun."

George Adsell turned and headed for the bar. He barged in between the girl and a man she had been talking to and the man took it, backed away. A little while later George and the girl headed for the back door. That was the most direct way to Flo's establishment, a house back of the saloon.

Justine finished his third drink, thought about another but decided against it. Then, while he waited for the return of the posse, he spent a little time thinking about Lillian. She had been nearly cold to him tonight. She had almost refused to talk to him. In a way he could understand how she felt. She had liked Tom Gallard, and most likely, she had seen him killed. A thing like that made an impression on a sensitive person. No wonder she had been so blunt with him. In another day or two she would get over the way she was feeling. Next time he came to town things might be different.

He heard some men ride in and he hurried outside. The posse was dismounting near the sheriff's office, up the street. If they had brought in a prisoner he could not pick him out. After a moment he headed in that direction. By the time he got there the posse had disbanded and Tanner was alone in his office. He had just lighted his lamp.

"So you didn't get him," Justine said, and there was a touch of anger in his voice.

Tanner looked around at him. "Nope, I didn't."

"Wasn't he there?"

"Yep. He was there."

"Then why the hell didn't you drag him in."

"Mrs. Gallard said she would need him until after the funeral."

"What!"

"Seemed reasonable to me," Tanner said. "Mrs. Gallard doesn't have any other men folks, an' Tom was kind of heavy. More 'n she can handle. Told her I'd bring Red in after the funeral. Anything wrong with that?"

"Plenty!" Justine snapped. "When I ask you to do somethin', I expect you to do it."

Tanner frowned, and he shook his head. "A lot of folks are gonna be upset about Gallard's death. I didn't want to make things any worse."

"Let me worry about that, huh? You bring in that Injun, right after the funeral. Understand?"

Tanner frowned, but then he asked, "You gonna make a charge against him? I went after him without one, but to make it legal I ought to have a warrant. The judge . . ."

"Just go get him," Justine said. "Hell with the warrant."

He swung away, headed back to the saloon, and he wondered why he felt so upset. Gallard was dead. That was the important thing to remember. The Injun kid Gallard had picked up a few years ago had made quite a play, gunning down Rossiter, but that really was not important. The Injun wouldn't last very long.

It started raining the night before the funeral. It was still raining in the morning. Red got up early. He started the kitchen fire. That was one of his chores, anyhow. There were two bedrooms in the house. The Gallards had used the large bedroom. Since he had come here, the other bedroom had been his. He was still staying there.

Myrt came into the kitchen while he was testing coffee. He poured her a cup and she carried it to the window and looked out. After a moment she shook her head. "I'm afraid we won't have many people for the funeral."

"The weather might clear up," Red said.

"I doubt it. It might rain all day."

"Some of the people who come, can come in here," Red said. "If there are too many for the house, the others can get shelter in the barn."

"There'll be a dozen people, at least. Maybe more. We can have the service here. I had hoped to have the service outside." Myrt smiled. "Tom liked the outdoors. It was his church."

The day before Red had prepared the grave. It was in a grove down near the river. It had been a quiet day yesterday. There had been a steady stream of visitors. Most had been ranch families but there had been a few people from town. No one had said very much, at least to Red. Some might have said more to Myrt, and probably had. Most who had stopped yesterday had said they would be here today, for the services, but the rain could change that.

They had breakfast, then Red went outside and took care of the horses, fed the chickens. The extra team and wagon had been picked up yesterday by Bernie Meyers. There were now seven horses in the corral. One was his, one would be used by Myrt, the five others would be taken over to Ingerhalls. They would be picked up this afternoon. The Ingerhalls would also take the chickens. There were two cages here, and Ingerhall could lend several more. It would not be too hard to move them. Myrt, herself, was going to move in with the Oldrings, temporarily. She would close the house, here — and hope nothing would happen to it. Red was supposed to head east, find a new life for himself.

This was the plan they had worked out yesterday. It was mostly Myrt's plan. She had worked out what to do with the horses, the chickens, and herself. And she had begged him to move east. It had been easier to agree with her than to argue.

Red took care of the morning chores. Then he took a little time, alone, in the barn, practicing with his hand gun. He used dummy shells so the weight of the gun would be right; he would holster his gun, whip it up and pull the trigger. He did that again and again and again. He tried it standing straight up. He tried it crouching, turning, falling, getting up, and in every position he could think of. This had been a routine practice up to yesterday. Since then he had been very serious about it. He was not going east, as Myrt wanted. And he was not going to hide himself in the mountains. He was not sure what he meant to do, but he would stay around here, somewhere. He had three secret hideout places here in the valley. It was time to use them.

He finished his practicing and went inside. Myrt was at the stove, cooking something. There were two huge coffee pots on the stove, getting warm. All the china had been set out on the table. Soon, two of the women would arrive and take over the kitchen work so Myrt could retire to the bedroom until it was time for services. He thought it was foolish to have to feed the people who came to the funeral, but that was the customary thing to do.

"Red?" Myrt called. "Have you moved your horse out of sight, down by the river and in the trees?"

"Not yet," Red answered.

"Then I think you'd better do that now — the horse and the things you want to take. I'll get you the thousand dollars."

"Later," Red said. "I'll move my horse now."

She looked at him frowning. "I want you to leave right after the services. We'll have to say goodbye to each other before the people get here."

"I know."

"Then hurry, Red. Move your horse into the trees then come back here."

"Soon as I can," Red said.

He went outside, crossed to the corral, caught his horse and saddled him, then he rode him down to the river and into the trees. When the horse was well out of sight of the house he dismounted, tied the horse loosely and headed back to the house. Three people who had come for the funeral were riding into the yard, the Oldrings. He hurried to take care of their horses. All three went inside.

A little while later the Ingerhalls arrived, Mike and Jolly. Their son, Chet, was not with them. They went inside. And right after that the Kreels rode in. They joined the others inside the house.

Red stayed outside. He knew he should have gone in but he didn't. He told himself he was waiting to look after the horses of any of the people who came, but more honestly, he was staying outside because he would have been uncomfortable in the house. There would have been quiet talk about Gallard. He didn't want to be quiet about Gallard. He wanted to do something about it.

No one else came for a time. The rain continued. Red sought shelter in the barn. He did some guessing about what he might do if the sheriff arrived and tried to arrest him. He imagined Justine raiding the funeral. He wouldn't, of course, but if he did . . .

A slight shrouded figure showed in the doorway, stood there, hesitant, then moved in a step or two. She threw back the covering over her head. It was Fran Oldring.

"I'm down here," Red called.

Fran stayed where she was. "Myrt wants to see you."

"Yes. I know."

"What should I tell her?"

"Why not say you couldn't find me?"

"That wouldn't be the truth."

"No, I guess it wouldn't," Red said. "What are they doing in there? Talking?"

"Mostly."

"I'm not good at talking."

"Neither am I," Fran said. "I just sit, and don't say anything."

"What do you think about?"

"I think about hundreds of things. Thousands. I could never tell you all the things I think about. There wouldn't be time."

He stared ahead, nodded. He thought he could understand her. He did a lot of thinking himself. It was probably about different things, but to an extent he and Fran Oldring were much alike.

"I guess you'll never be able to finish gentling my horse," Fran said.

"What ever gave you that idea," Red said scowling. "When I start a job, I finish it."

She took several steps forward but stopped. "How can you? Father says if you don't get away, then Justine's men will ride you down."

"They might try. If I had a horse like yours they'd never catch me."

The girl bit her lips. She looked away. "Do you want him? Night?"

"Do I want him!" Red stood up. "I'd give anything in the world for a horse like him."

"If you had a horse like Night, could you stay here in the valley? I mean . . ."

"I'm going to stay here, anyhow."

"Then you can have him, Red."

He took a quick breath and looked at her, then looked away. Did she really mean what she had said, that he could have her horse? Surely she didn't mean it.

"You haven't ridden him yet," Fran said, "but I guess you can. Father says you know how to talk to him."

"So could you, if you tried."

"Do you really think I could?"

He nodded but scowled, and he said, "You didn't mean it, did you? That I could have Night?"

"That's what I said, isn't it?"

"How much?"

"I guess you ought to pay what Father paid for the horse. I think he paid fifty dollars. Do you have that much?"

"More, in the bank. But Night is worth more than fifty dollars."

"Then pay me what you think is right. Are you coming in to see Myrt?"

"In a little while." He raised his head. "Don't you hear someone riding in?"

She listened but shook her head. "I only hear the rain. And I better go in. I'll tell Myrt you'll be in, soon."

"Yes. I'll be in soon."

"And you'll pick up your horse — when you can?"

"When I can. And thanks, Fran. I wish . . ."

"I want to see you ride him," Fran said. "And some day, as part payment, I want to ride him. Just once. Is that all right?"

"I owe you more than that," Red said.

She nodded, turned away. At the door she stopped to cover her head then she moved into the rain, running.

Toward eleven o'clock more people rode in and as the clock moved toward twelve it seemed that they were going to have a good crowd for the services. All the nearby neighbors were here, and there were a few who had come from far down the valley. There might have been a dozen from the town. The sheriff was among the dozen. Red's heart had jumped when he saw him, but nothing in particular happened. Maybe the sheriff would not try anything until after the funeral service.

Four more people rode in at about ten minutes to twelve. There were several more just before then and just after, but these four caught Red's particular attention. He stiffened when he saw them. He couldn't believe what he was seeing, but unless he was mistaken, here was Ben Justine, his daughter Kathy, and two of his men, George Adsell and Joe Stubbs.

The four rode in as a compact group. Justine looked straight ahead, his lips tight and unsmiling. Kathy was frowning, she seemed mad about something. George Adsell wore his usual scowl. Joe Stubbs, a small, thin man, middle aged, hunched in the saddle. He seemed tired but then he always seemed tired.

Red took a look at the four people, and another look, and still another. He shook his head, not wanting to believe that Justine could have the nerve to come to Gallard's funeral. He hardly noticed Kathy or the other men. He lumped them together with Justine. What was he doing here, mourning at Gallard's funeral? How did he have the gall to appear? He reached for the gun he was wearing.

Oldring, who had come outside and was standing in the rain not far away, spoke quickly but under his breath. "Easy, Red. Don't reach for your gun. I guess Justine had the right to come here, no matter what you think of him."

"He had no right at all," Red answered.

"Go on inside," Oldring said. "You ought to be standing with Myrt when Justine shows up, to pay his respects."

"I'd rather spit at him."

"Don't," Oldring said. "At least, don't do it this time. Stand with Myrt — and let her do the talking."

"Stand with Myrt," Oldring had said. "Let her do the talking." Red nodded. He remembered the way Myrt had talked to the sheriff. She had done pretty well. She was no frail woman, easy to push over. She stood up for what she believed in. He looked toward Justine, his daughter and the three men. They were dismounting. In another moment they would be heading for the house.

"Go ahead," Oldring said. "I want you to stand straight."

"I'll stand straight," Red said, and he headed for the house.

The place was crowded but he had no trouble finding Myrt. She had changed clothes. She was wearing a black dress but there was nothing over her head, no veil to hide her face. She looked pale, but composed. He moved straight toward her.

"Red, I've been waiting for you." She smiled, and reached out and put her hand on his arm.

"Justine's here," he said under his breath. "And his daughter and two of his men."

"I'm not much surprised," Myrt said. "Will you stand with me?"

"I'll stand with you," Red said.

86

Oldring had said to stand straight. He stood straighter than ever before. He stood with pride. There was nothing impassive in his expression. He didn't even watch the door.

CHAPTER
SIX

There was a low hum of conversation running through the room, but the sounds faded, stopped. Red was aware of that. He knew why. Justine had entered the room. Few would have guessed he had hired Rossiter, but everyone present must have known that he and Gallard had not been friends. It was hard to understand why he was here.

Red, with Myrt close at his side, turned to face him. He had left his daughter and his two men outside. He had entered the room alone, and now he came directly toward Myrt. He did not even look at Red. He never did so far as people could see. That had been his way of treating him — never to admit that he existed.

The man was big, wide shouldered and heavy. He was always neatly dressed. Today, he managed a faint smile as he stood in front of Myrt, and he said, "Mrs. Gallard, I'm sorry about what happened to your husband. We didn't agree on a good many things but he was a fine man."

"Thank you, Mr. Justine," Myrt said quietly.

He had put out his hand but she ignored it, did not seem to notice it. Red took a look at her face. Her lips were tight but she was staring straight at the men.

"If there's anything I can do for you, just let me know," Justine said.

"I think you've done enough for me," Myrt said.

He blinked, didn't seem to know what to say next.

Myrt spoke again. "This is my son, Red."

"Huh! Your son?" Justine gulped. A flush of color showed in his face. He turned and looked at Red. He almost had to.

Red nodded. "Hello, Justine."

A sound came from somewhere in Justine's throat. He stared at Red for a moment, muttered something under his breath and turned away, headed for the door. No one stopped him. No one else said anything. He reached the door, opened it, stepped outside and closed it.

Almost at once a hum of conversation picked up. Red heard several mentions of Justine's name. Probably, everyone here was wondering why he had come. That was what they were asking each other.

"You should have come in earlier," Myrt said. "I wanted another chance to talk to you before you left. And I want to give you the money."

"I won't be leaving right away," Red answered.

"But I want you to. It won't be safe to wait."

"I'll seem to leave but then I'll come back later, after dark."

"I was going to leave with the Oldrings, right after the services."

"Then I'll see you at Oldrings."

Myrt was frowning. "You haven't — you haven't changed your mind about leaving. Red, if you don't . . ."

"I know. It won't be safe to stay here." He managed a rare smile. "Don't worry about me, Myrt. I'm not going to be foolish."

He started to turn away but Myrt called, "They're going to have services right away."

He nodded. "I just want to get a drink."

He turned and headed for the kitchen, moved close to the kitchen door.

Others crowded in. The services started. Red listened to the singing, then he listened to what the preacher had to say but he didn't listen carefully. He knew Gallard better than the preacher, knew more what he had been like. He could sense his value as a man. He didn't need to listen to what was being said. When he thought the preacher was nearly through he opened the kitchen door, stepped outside, and closed it.

The rain had slackened but it had not stopped. It was a grey, wet day, a little chilly. A few men had not crowded into the house. Some were standing in the scant shelter of the barn building, a few were standing just inside the open doors. Among these was Justine, his daughter and the two men who had come with him. Red was surprised they had not left.

He turned up the collar of his coat, put on his hat, stepped out in the yard and headed down the yard. This was the way to the grove, where Gallard would be buried — but from there he could move on into a heavier stand of timber and to the place where he had left his horse. If anyone asked him where he was going he would say he wanted to be sure the grave was ready. In a way, he was responsible for that.

90

He started down the yard but he had taken only a few steps before someone called, "Hey, Injun! Wait a minute."

He slowed down, stopped, and he thought, at first, that it had been Justine who called him but when he turned and looked toward the barn doorway he saw it was another man who had stepped out and was walking toward him, Joe Stubbs.

Red scarcely knew the man. He was asking himself: "What does he want of me? We never had words. Unless Justine's the one who sent him out to . . ."

Justine, his daughter and George Adsell were still with the others in the shelter of the barn, looking out No one else had followed Joe Stubbs.

The man got closer. He stopped. And he asked, "Where you think you're goin', Injun?"

Red answered as he had planned. "This is the way to the grave, I just want to be sure that everything's ready."

"Then you ain't runnin' away, huh?"

"Away from where?"

"Away from me," Stubbs turned his head to spit. At the same time he took his hands out of his pockets, unbuttoned his Slicker and coat. Maybe he was overheated, or maybe he wanted to be sure he could get to his holstered gun in a hurry, if he wanted to.

"I don't know what you mean," Red said.

He was not wearing a slicker. His holster was lower than the bottom edge of his coat. His muscles had tightened up but that probably didn't show. He stood waiting to see what Stubbs meant to do.

"Jules Rossiter was a friend of mine," Stubbs said. "Did you know that?"

Red shook his head. "Nope. I didn't."

"I want to talk to you about that," Stubbs said. "Want to meet me in town, tonight?"

"Nope. I don't."

"Scared?"

"Nope. Why don't you do your talking now?"

The man had stiffened. "Huh! Now!"

"That's what I said." Red was watching him narrowly. "Why put it off? What have you got to say?"

"I talk with my gun," Stubbs grated.

Red nodded. "Any time you're ready, go ahead."

He should not have done this, he knew. This was going to be a harsh interruption to Gallard's funeral. People who could blame him for this would do it. Even Myrt might not like it, but it was too late to think about that now.

He took a quick look past Stubbs toward the house and the barn. No one else had left the house, the preacher must have had a second wind, must still be talking. Those in the shelter of the barn and inside of it were looking this way, watching closely. No one else had joined them.

Stubbs had hunched over, he seemed smaller. His arm bowed out from the shoulder and his hand was supposed to be like a striking serpent. His hand would grab the gun, whip it out of its holster, lift it and fire it.

The man moved. He got as far as lifting the gun from its holster. He had started raising it when a bullet from

Red's gun smashed through his chest. That drove him backwards. His knees folded and he smashed to the ground, and stayed there.

Red looked at him, looked away. He lowered his gun, holstered it then looked again at the barn. Justine had stepped outside. George Adsell had joined him but both men stopped. They did not move any closer. Several other men gathered around them. There were sounds from the house, too. Several men had come outside.

Red thought, "Maybe they'll stop me, maybe they won't. We'll see what happens." He turned and moved on down the yard. No one called him. There were no shots. He kept moving. Soon he was at the edge of the grove. A few more steps and he was out of sight of anyone at the house.

Justine was startled when Joe Stubbs squared up to the Indian. This was not supposed to happen. Stubbs had been supposed to throw a challenge, make a date to see Red in town. He had not wanted any trouble here. If he had to explain Red's death . . .

There was a shot — just one shot. It had come from Red's gun. It was Joe Stubbs who was staggering backwards, dropping to the ground. He had not moved fast enough. What had been wrong with him? He had been supposed to be one of the fastest men in the country.

He looked at George Adsell, who was shaking his head, who seemed startled.

Someone who was nearby, spoke. "Never saw anything faster in my life. Stubbs didn't even have a chance."

"The Injun drew first," Justine said flatly.

"Nope he didn't," someone else said. "If anyone moved first, it was Stubbs."

"Who said that?" Justine snapped.

"I did." It was Roy Cosgriff who was talking. "I don't want to fight about it, but that's the way I saw it."

Several others nodded. Justine hesitated. He could raise the issue again and some of these men might back down, but this was a foolish thing to fight about.

He turned to George Adsell. "Go see how badly Joe's been hurt."

George nodded, moved out into the rain. Several others joined him and several from the house headed to where Stubbs was lying. Among them was the sheriff.

Justine looked away. He was thinking of what he would say when Kathy spoke: "Why, Father? Why?"

He glanced at her. "We'll talk later, on the way home."

"No, I want to know now." Her voice was louder. "Did you know this was going to happen?"

"Of course not."

"Then why did you bring Joe Stubbs with you? Why do you hire men like him — killers? Why did we come out here? You never liked Mr. Gallard."

A wave of anger swept across him. "Will you shut up, Kathy! I came here out of respect to Gallard. You don't understand."

She shook her head. "I surely don't. I think I'll go home."

She turned and started outside, a tall, slender blond. Her blue eyes looked very angry.

"Kathy, you wait for me," Justine shouted.

She did not answer, did not look back. It was not far to where her horse had been tied. She reached him, untied him, swung into the saddle and rode away through the rain.

Justine watched her. He thought of calling her again but he was afraid she would not answer. It was better for his pride to let her go than to make this seem important. What was he going to do about her? He was not sure. He was not even sure why they fought with each other. He should not have brought her today. This had been another mistake. He should have left her behind and he should not have brought Stubbs — or maybe that had been wise. He knew, now, just about how good the Indian was with a gun. Too good. What did he call himself? Red Pardee? That was too fancy a name for an Indian. He would never call him that.

George came back to the barn. He was shaking his head. "That damned Injun! Joe's dead."

"Load him on his horse," Justine said, "We'll head back."

George nodded, turned away. His place was taken by Dave Tanner. He lowered his voice. "Want me to go after him?"

"Do I have to tell you what to do?" Justine snapped. "Ain't you the sheriff?"

"Sure but . . ."

"All right, go after him or let him go. What the hell do I care?" He moved past Tanner, stepped out into the rain.

A crowd had come out of the house. Among them were six men carrying the pine box coffin that held Gallard's body. They started down the yard, toward the grove on the river. The crowd was forming up-trail, behind them. He reminded himself of what was happening. This was the end of Tom Gallard. That was the important thing to remember. Who cared about the Injun with the fancy name?

He noticed Myrt and it occurred to him he might say something to her, explain that the recent shooting had not been his fault. But why should he worry about that? He had come here hoping to seem friendly, so that later it might be easier to deal with her when he offered to buy the ranch. She might have known that her husband had not liked him but that was not important, now that he was gone. In a week or a month, if things in the valley looked bad, Myrt would be glad to sell the ranch for anything she could get. He had worried about her but that was foolish. As a matter of fact, he should not have come to the funeral. He was pushing too hard. The thing to do was to slow down.

He straightened, nodded, walked to where he had left his horse. George Adsell was there. He had borrowed help to get Joe Stubbs lifted across his horse. He was now tying the body in place. The man who had helped him had moved away. There was no one else nearby.

"I thought you said Stubbs was good with his gun," Justine muttered.

"Thought so myself," George said.

"But now?"

"That damned Injun! He couldn't be that good."

"Want to try him?"

"Not if I don't have to."

"Get the men after him. Take the five hundred dollars you were going to give to Stubbs and hand it over to the man who nails the Injun. Don't take a chance with him."

George grunted.

"You can head for home," Justine said. "I want to stop in town for a few minutes. If you see my daughter . . ."

"What?"

"Never mind," Justine said, "I'll tell her myself. I'll tell her plenty."

Kathy Justine would be twenty in another month, and in another month she was supposed to travel east to Philadelphia, to the Havenhill Academy. This was a school restricted to girls who had good breeding and whose parents had plenty of money. Kathy had never been sure on what basis she had been accepted. She had spent two years at the Academy. In two more years she would be finished. That meant, in two more years she would be ready to move out into society, but she was not sure whether that meant Philadelphia's society or the society of Dry Fork, Arizona. She had learned some things at the Academy, some good things and some that were not so good.

She did not quite understand her conflict with her father. She disagreed with him on nearly everything that came up. Now and then she told herself that part of the blame was hers, but she really didn't mean it. Today, she had not wanted to go to the Gallard funeral. She knew about them but she had never met them, and she was sure that the man who had been killed had not been one of her father's friends. She had gone today, trying to be nice. She had gone because her father asked her to, but after what had happened, she wished she had stayed away. The rain and the cold made her miserable. The sudden shooting in the yard had startled her. She did not like violence. She didn't care for most of the men who worked for her father. Particularly she disliked George Adsell, who would have slobbered all over her if she had let him. If it had not been for one particular person in the valley she would have been looking forward to another year in the Havenhill Academy.

That one particular person caught up with her shortly after she left the Gallard ranch. He pulled up, and grinned at her through the rain. He said, "Hello there, Kathy. Mind if I ride with you?"

She shook her head and her eyes were suddenly sparkling. "Of course not, but Father might catch up with us."

"I'll keep looking back," Ed Cooper said.

He was twenty-one, tall, thin and sandy haired. Kathy liked him — he was reckless, impudent, challenging — but she was a little afraid of him at the same time. He worked as a cowhand for Fred Kreel and that did not put him very high in her father's estimation of people. She had reminded him that she had little choice of companionship around here, but that had not helped.

"Were you at Gallard's?" she asked bluntly.

"Yes, I was there." He looked back over his shoulder. "I was in the house."

"That's why I didn't see you," Kathy said. "I didn't go in the house. Father did but he didn't stay."

"Did you see the shooting?"

She nodded. "It was horrible. I wish I hadn't watched."

"How did it happen? Who started it?"

"I don't know. Red — is that his name? Red?"

"Yes, Red Pardee."

"He came out of the house and started walking toward the river. Joe Stubbs shouted at him, and he stopped. Then Joe went out to where he was waiting. There was some talking, then Joe grabbed his gun. Red shot him — just like that. Then he turned and left."

"That's two for the Indian. Rossiter, then Joe Stubbs."

"Why do you call him Indian? Isn't he part white?"

"Half white, but in this part of the country if you're part Indian, then you might as well be all Indian. At least, lots of folks feel that way. Your father does."

"I know how father feels, but I don't have to feel the same way, do I?"

"I guess not." He looked at her narrowly. "Do you know the Indian?"

"No. And he's not an Indian."

"He won't be around very long. Somebody'll get him."

"Why?"

He grinned, shook his head. "Why do we have to talk about him? I'd rather talk about us. How about getting married?"

She looked away but she was flushing. "You don't mean that. I know you don't."

"But I do. We could head for Mesa City. Or Tucson? How would that be?"

"How about here?" Kathy said.

"Huh? You mean here in Dry Fork."

"There's a preacher in Dry Fork. We could even wait for him on the road. He was at Gallard's. Do you want to do that?"

He scowled at her. "Now you're the one who doesn't mean it."

"Why don't I?" She was suddenly sure of herself. "Why don't we get married right here in Dry Fork?"

"Your father might not like it."

"Does that bother you?"

"It could be a complication. It would be a lot easier to head out to some other town."

"We'd have to come back."

"Nope. Not right away. I could get a job most anywhere. But I just wonder — do you mean it, that we could get married here?"

100

She looked straight at him and she tried to be honest. "I don't know, Ed. I'm not sure I'm ready to be married, but I won't run away. I am certain of that."

His voice had changed. It was lower. "What if I said we'd get married here?"

"We both better think about it."

"All right, we'll think about it," Ed said. "And I want you, not your father's ranch. Understand?"

"It would have to be that way."

"Good," Ed said. "I'm gonna plan on it. We'll see what happens."

They rode on through the rain, and it seemed the rain was not so bad. Kathy straightened up. She didn't think she had fallen in love with Ed Cooper, but she liked him better than ever before. Maybe he could stand up to her father. She was not at all sure he could, but if he did it would be interesting. If she ever got married she would expect her husband to tower over her father. At least, that was what she thought she wanted — if she wasn't asking for too much.

CHAPTER
SEVEN

Red had not stopped at the open grave. He kept walking to where he had left his horse, hidden in the trees, and he meant to mount up and start riding. He did that, but not right away. He stopped when he reached his horse, looked back and listened. He could hear no one following him, but it was reasonable that someone might. Back there near the house, a little while ago, he had drawn his gun and killed a man. At the moment he did, Joe Stubbs had been reaching for his own gun, and he would have fired it. From the standpoint of self-defense, he could justify what he had done, but the interesting thing to him was this: he could have avoided the gun duel, but he had made no attempt to do it. In fact he had provoked it. Joe Stubbs had suggested that they meet in town. Red could have agreed. He could even have dodged a meeting in town but such a possibility never occurred to him. Instead, he had welcomed this chance to hit back at Justine.

Was that what he had done? Probably. Stubbs had worked for Justine, had represented Justine. In blasting him down, Red had really been slamming at Justine. He thought, now: "What do I have against Joe Stubbs? Nothing, even if he was a friend of Rossiters. I've got to get my thinking straight. To hate Justine, do I have to hate everyone who rides for him?"

He thought about that for a moment. If Justine's riders stood by him, then that seemed to put them in the same class. What about Kathy? The same would be true of her.

He mounted his horse, started off through the trees bordering the river. After a time he crossed the stream and a little while later he cut out into the open country. He knew the valley from one end to the other, from the north ridge to the desert edge to the south. He knew the river, the creeks, the forest lands, and the meadows, the rock flats, the chaparral, the mesquite thickets. He felt at home, anywhere. He was heading west, toward Justine's part of the valley, but he did not worry about that. He would soon move into the trees bordering the river. He had a hideout spot up here, a very good one, but he did not plan to go near it. This place, and the other hideouts, were for an emergency.

He reined up, finally, dismounted, watered and tied his horse; then he settled down on a flat, sheltered rock, close to the stream. He had spent four hours getting here, in a rather circular way. There were three more hours of light — three hours to wait. Red thought of what he might do after it got dark. It was only five miles from here to the Justine ranch. He knew exactly where it was, and although he had never been there, he knew it well from a distance. He knew how the buildings were arranged, what they were. He knew there were two dogs at the ranch. They barked at everyone so they would bark at him if he got too close. He did not plan to get too close — tonight. Some other time he might have to.

It had stopped raining. It was still cloudy but the clouds were high. By morning it might be clear. It might even turn warm again. The earth was still fairly soft. If he rode toward the Justine ranch tonight he would leave a marked trail, but what if he left his horse behind — what then?

This was a time for one of his rare smiles. He was going to pay a distant visit to the Justine ranch, tonight, and in the morning Justine's riders would go crazy trying to pick up his trail. They might do that at the river when it was light but he doubted that they would look this far away.

He had brought some food and while he waited for the dark he had a cold meal. He had already changed from boots to moccasins. That was what he would wear on his feet tonight. There was good grass just beyond the river. The moccasins would leave only a faint trail and by morning the grass would have straightened up and would not show where he had been. There would be no trail.

As soon as it was dark he headed for the Justine ranch, and he hurried, moved at a jog trot. It took only a little while to come in sight of the clustering lights of the main building and the bunkhouse. He slowed down and listened. There was nothing to hear but the low song of the wind. He moved closer to the ranch, much closer. Now, he could see the individual lamplit windows, and crouching down he used the rifle he had brought with him, fired six shots. He smashed four windows in the main building, and two of the windows of the bunkhouse. Then he got up, started circling the place.

The lights in the main building and in the bunkhouse were turned off, almost at once, and some of the men must have rushed outside. He could hear them shouting at each other, probably asking each other what had happened. Where had those six shots come from? Who was responsible?

Red stopped again, crouched down. He peered toward the ranch. It was still a cloudy night. He could make out the main ranch buildings but only as deeper shadows. He had reloaded his rifle and now, carefully, he aimed at the space between the main building and the bunkhouse, and he raked that area with bullets. He fired quickly and the instant he emptied his rifle, he got up and moved on, circled farther around the ranch.

There was more yelling from the ranch yard but he doubted he had hit anyone. Maybe a dozen shots were fired in his direction. Most were high. None came very near. The men at the ranch could not have seen him, they could only guess about where he was. There might have been flashes from his gun but he had kept close to the ground.

He reloaded the rifle again, smashed two bullets into the main building, moved on and fired again then circled back the other way, stopped and emptied the rifle. By now there was some steady firing from the ranch. Two shots came fairly close to him, but that was accidental.

Red moved back to a point opposite to where he had first fired. He reloaded the rifle, and emptied it, every shot aimed at the main building. He moved once more, half circled the ranch, then dropped down into the deep grass and waited to see what might happen.

In the next ten minutes maybe a hundred shots were wasted, fired blindly into the darkness, but gradually the firing slackened, then stopped. Red could not see what was happening at the ranch but he could guess what the men were thinking. There had been no more shots at the ranch for quite a time. Maybe the man who had been firing the shots had gone. They might even have guessed who the man was. That should have been easy.

Red stayed where he was. In about fifteen more minutes he heard the sounds of horses and he raised his head, listened, and searched the shadows toward the ranch. Three men had saddled and mounted their horses. No, there were four men. He caught a glimpse of them but then lost them in the shadows. The men had started south but then turned east. Red waited and listened. The men had turned again, headed north. By this time he could guess what they were doing: circling the ranch. Before very long they would pass close to him. They might even ride over him, find him.

He rolled over on his face, turned toward the approaching men. He was still close to the ground; most of his body was hidden in the grass but he was tense, ready to move if he had to. The men might not come near him, or, from a short distance away, his prone body might look like an outcropping rock. If the men came closer than that he might have a fight on his hands.

The horses were nearer. He could suddenly see them. He thought for an instant that they were headed straight for him but then they veered nearer to the ranch. They would miss him, but not by very much. As they passed him they might see him, but if he stayed motionless they might not see him as a person. He could be glad, now, for the darkness of the cloudy night.

He pulled off his hat, pushed it under his chest. He drew the rifle closer so it would be hidden by his body and he lowered his head, and after that he did not move again. He listened to the sound of the horses and to the mutterings of one of the men but he couldn't hear what the man was saying. The horses came nearer, they came even to where he was lying, they moved on. In another moment they were moving away.

Red waited another half minute, then he relaxed, turned to his side, mopped his face. He was thinking: "I shouldn't have stayed. I should have left, long ago. I wanted to do this, declare myself. In a way I have but I want to do more. I want Justine to remember this." He was not sure Justine was there, but he hoped he was. At least, he would hear about what had happened tonight, and he was not going to like it. If there was going to be any raiding, Justine would order it. It was not in his plan that anyone should ever attack him.

The four riders returned to the ranch. Red watched that from a distance. He had to guess what the men had reported, probably that the man who had been pouring shots at the ranch had fled. Someone would have said that in the morning they would pick up the trail of the man who had attacked the ranch, but that was highly questionable. In the morning Justine's men might find several of the places where the man had stopped and they would find some empty shells. They might find traces of his moccasins but they wouldn't be able to follow his trail. He could be sure of that.

It was half an hour before there were any lights at the ranch; then one light showed up in the bunkhouse, a very dim light. When nothing happened the light was turned higher and a little while later lamplight was turned on in the main building.

Red sat up. He put his hat back on, reached for his rifle, stretched out on the ground again, aimed carefully and started firing. He smashed out three more windows. The rest of the shots in the rifle were hammered at the main door.

The lights were turned off again. By that time Red was moving. He reloaded the rifle, stopped and emptied it, and moved on again. He did that again and again. On his last move now, he hugged the earth again and reloaded the rifle. Shots were spattering out from the ranch buildings. Blind shots. There was only a chance one might hit him but after a time, most likely, those four riders, or maybe more, would ride out and start looking for him. They would be more careful this time, they would look harder. The wise thing for him to do was to back off.

He waited until the firing slackened and stopped, then he got up, turned away. He backed off maybe half a mile then sat down and waited.

He heard the men searching the area around the ranch. The men made another circling trip. Then, maybe, some of the men settled down in the darkness. If he had been Justine, that was what he would have ordered. He would have put out silent guards. He would have had them stationed all around the ranch, used every man he had. He would have told the men to wait and to watch for the return of the man who had attacked the ranch.

Red looked in the direction of the ranch. He listened but there was nothing to hear. He moved in nearer, looked again and listened. He changed positions again but he did this carefully, he kept close to the ground. In the next hour he heard nothing, he saw nothing. He waited another hour, and another, then he moved in, slowly, taking his time. He stiffened, once. He thought he heard someone off to the left but he was not sure about that. The undefinable sound he had heard was not repeated. After a long wait he moved on.

There were no lights in the main building ahead, nor were there any lights in the bunkhouse. There should not have been any lights. It was long past midnight, it was moving toward dawn. Everyone at the ranch should have been asleep. That is, everyone except the guards — if there were any guards. He was soon going to be finding out.

He was flat to the earth but he raised his rifle, aimed at the front of the building and started firing. He pumped the rifle and fired again. He sent a third shot at the building and as he did that he heard a shout from the side and he lowered his rifle, looked that way.

"He's over here!" a man was shouting. "Dave! Ellery! Bert! Get over here!"

Red could see the man vaguely, a bulky, moving figure almost shrouded in the shadows. A bullet from the man's gun streaked above him. Another bullet was lower. He swung his rifle that way and fired it and the man yelled. He threw up his arms, seemed to stagger back and go down, merge into the shadows. He might have moved after that, but Red could not see him. Nor could he see Dave, Ellery or Bert, whoever they were. Red took a quick look from side to side. He even looked behind but there was no one there.

For the moment no one was bothering him. He could have sent a few more bullets at the ranch buildings but it might be better to move out. Dave, Ellery, and Bert might show up on their horses. He didn't expect that, but it would be wise to get away while he could. He got up, turned away, and started running, heading to the south. In a little while he would curve to the west, then to the north, then to the east.

No one followed him, and once he was away, he was sure no one would. He doubted that even a good tracker could have followed him for more than a quarter of a mile.

It was still dark when he reached the river but within an hour it would start to grow light. Red had some water, then he sat down and thought about what had happened. This had been a successful night. He might not have frightened anyone at the Justine ranch, but at least he had been annoying. He had smothered the lights; and twice when Justine's crowd thought he had

110

fled, they discovered he was still around. After his second attack they had posted guards, and one had been hurt. When Justine heard about it, or if he had been there, he would be raging. He would guess who was responsible, that ought to make him more angry. He would have his men out in the morning, early, and when they were unable to pick up his trail Justine might send them out in a valleywide search.

What might that mean? This was a long and wide valley. It would take almost two days to ride it from one end to the other. It would take most of a day to ride across it. There were scores of wooded areas where a man could hide. His men could ride for a week and not begin to do a good search. Of course, while his men were doing that, they could not move against anyone else. A search would be a crippling thing. The night had been worthwhile.

He moved down the river. He passed the sheltered rock where he had eaten and waited the night before, and went on to the place where he had left his horse. He stopped there, briefly, and had a cold meal. Then he saddled up and slanted across the valley in the direction of the Oldrings.

It was late in the afternoon before he reached Seven Mile Gulch. The gulch was a break in the north edge of the valley. It was only a little more than half a mile deep and half that wide. A small stream ran through it. Part of the gulch had good grass; beyond the grass was scrub oak and juniper and even a few pines. A man could ride out of the gulch almost anywhere. The walls were not steep.

Oldring had only about a hundred cattle. He could not have pastured many more. He had two good bulls. Above the house was the garden and it was rather extensive. Oldring had said many times that he was more of a farmer than a cattleman. Actually, he was both.

There was a drift fence across the mouth of the gulch. This kept his cattle out of the valley. He had no herding problems. Red could have bypassed the fence and ridden in from the side but in crossing the valley he came to the road, and he followed it, opened the gate Oldring had set up, then closed it. In a few more minutes he was dismounting near the corral.

Myrt and Sally must have heard him ride in. They showed up on the porch when he turned that way. Oldring was working in the potato patch, just above the house. Fran was beyond him. Both waved and started toward the house.

Myrt spoke from the porch. "I suppose you know I've been worried to death about you."

"I'm sorry about that," Red said. "I couldn't have come much earlier."

"You must be starved," Sally said. "We'll have an early supper."

"I want to take another look at Fran's horse," Red said.

"Your horse." Sally said. "I'm glad she said you could have him. He's a man's horse."

Oldring and Fran were moving into the yard and Oldring called, "Howdy there, Red. You're looking fine."

Red nodded.

Before he could say anything Fran asked, "Are you going to try to ride your horse?"

"I want to see him, anyhow," Red said. "He's not my horse, really." He looked at Oldring. "Fran said . . ."

"I know what she said," Oldring replied. "He was her horse. If she wants you to have him that's the way we'll work it out. I'll bet anything he's expecting you."

"Yes, I think he is," Red said. "Let's go find out."

They trooped, down to the old corral. Night saw them coming. He danced to the far-side fence, snorted in defiance. Red moved part way toward him. He started talking to him. "Howdy there, Night. Been waiting for me? Sure you have, I know you have. And here I am, just like you knew I'd be."

He climbed over the rail, leaned back against it, went on talking.

Night snorted, reared up into the air, pounded down at the earth. He dashed halfway to where Red was standing but veered away and circled back to where he had been.

"Oldring, do you mind going to get my saddle and saddle blanket," Red said. His voice had not changed. He sounded as though he was talking to the horse. "I should have remembered them myself."

"I'll get them right away," Oldring said.

When he came back, Red was still talking to the horse. Oldring put the blanket over the top rail. He propped the saddle nearby.

"Thanks," Red said. "We're going to see what Night thinks about the blanket."

He reached for it, draped it over his arm, started toward the horse. Night reared up again, and again, and again. Red stopped, but then he moved on, turned a little to the side, reached out and put his hand on the horse's neck. Night trembled, but he stayed where he was.

"We're doing fine, fine," Red said "I haven't hurt you, have I? And I never will. Now, I'm going to put my blanket over your back, just put it there, that's all. You won't mind it a bit."

He moved the blanket very slowly, lifted it, fitted it across the horse's back. Then he patted the blanket lightly.

"How's that?" he said quietly. "You can hardly feel it. This blanket . . ."

He kept talking. He spent ten more minutes with the horse. He went to get the saddle and he put the saddle on the blanket but he didn't cinch it in place, and after only a moment he took the saddle and the blanket away. He thought that was enough for today.

"You could have gone farther," Oldring said. "I think you could have ridden him."

"Maybe, but he wasn't ready for that." Red said. "If I could spend a week, getting him ready . . ."

"A week?" Oldring said. "I'm afraid that — you can't stay here. I mean, it wouldn't be safe."

"Are you thinking about the sheriff or are you thinking about Justine?"

"I'm thinking about you, Red. Sure you can stay here. I can even insist on your right to stay here, but if Justine knew you were here he would just brush me aside."

"And it might be rough on Sally, too. And Myrt and Fran."

Oldring looked at his hands, and nodded. He asked, "How do you fight a cyclone? That's what we're up against. Justine's got too many guns. He owns the law, too. The local law, Dave Tanner. A man ought to be able to appeal to the law but you can't when the law's been corrupted. That's the way things are here."

They reached the house, and Sally said, "You men can sit out here on the porch. For a few minutes I'll need Fran and Myrt inside. We're going to have an early supper."

"I'll talk to you later, Red," Myrt said.

"No hurry," Red said.

"I still have your money."

"We'll talk about that."

"I want you to take it, Red. My husband would have approved. You know he would."

He looked away. "I'm still here, Myrt."

"But you can't stay here. You know you can't." She turned to Oldring. "Talk to him, please?"

"Sure. I'll do the best I can," Oldring said.

He took one of the chairs, a rocker, and he leaned back. He looked relaxed but he was frowning. Red took a look at him. Oldring was not a very large man, he did not look imposing. He had rounded shoulders, well-muscled arms. His hands were big and calloused. He had dark eyes, thin, tight lips and a small nose. He had not shaved today but he probably would tomorrow. Right now he showed some grey bristles on his chin and throat.

"What happened at the funeral, after I left?" Red asked.

"We finished it," Oldring said. "There wasn't much said about Stubbs' death. A dozen men said he went for his gun. Even Justine didn't raise a row. But Tanner did. He told Myrt and he told me that he wanted you in Dry Fork. He says there's got to be a hearing about Rossiter's death. If I see you I'm supposed to bring you in. That's his idea about what I ought to do."

"What's going to happen now?"

"You mean, what's Justine going to do? I think he's going to crowd in on Fred Kreel, Sam Weiler, or Mike Ingerhall. Or maybe two of them. Or maybe all three. Mike isn't so sure. Fred Kreel hopes for the best. Weiler seems most worried; but no one seems to have any notion about what to do. I talked to York. He doesn't live far from here. He says he's gonna stall, see if he can ride this out. How do you ride out a cyclone?"

"What about you?"

"I can be squeezed out any time. I'm not out in the valley. Justine can move in on me any time he wants to." He shook his head, looked from side to side. "I like this place, it's just my size. I can handle the work alone. I make enough to get by. My herds are getting better.

In a few more years I might even be making money —
but Justine can stop all that."

"I wouldn't let him."

"How would you stop him?"

"If the ranchers in the valley would get together . . ."

"Maybe, but they won't. Tom Gallard could have
pulled them together. Most of them respected him, and
they liked him. Of course that's why he was killed.
Justine had to get rid of him."

"If that could be proved . . ."

"We probably can't. Red, I want to ask you
something. What would you think if I disappeared for a
couple of weeks — just dropped out of sight?"

"Where would you go?"

"To Prescott, the capital of the Territory. I have some
friends there. I think they might listen to me, and they
might be able to influence the governor. We need help.
I don't know where else we can go."

"If you left, what about the women?"

"They want to stay here."

"Alone!"

"They don't think they would be in danger and
maybe they are right. Justine doesn't want trouble. He
wants to take over the valley, and with no more fighting
than is necessary. He wouldn't want to make war on
three women."

Red sat down. He stared at the rugged slope, off to
the south. He thought about what Oldring was
suggesting. Maybe he could get help from the outside
but he was not at all sure about that. And he didn't like
thinking about Myrt, Fran, and Sally, being left alone.

If he could stay here that might be the solution, but it was foolish to think that he could stay here. In fact, if he stayed here they would be in greater danger.

"Most times, we're not fair to our women," Oldring said. "Sally is a better shot than I am, and she's got a sharper temper. Myrt has been a good shot for years. I didn't want Fran to grow up with firearms, but she did, and she's damned good with a rifle. She's quick and strong. So are the other two. They could put up quite a fight, if they had to. I don't want that to happen but I don't think it will."

"Then, when are you leaving?" Red asked.

"In the morning, early. Or maybe I should leave tonight. No reason I shouldn't."

"I shouldn't stay here either," Red said.

"No. Some of Justine's men will be by. If you were here it might be harder on the women."

"I didn't plan to stay," Red said. "I wanted to see Myrt and I was interested in the horse. Maybe I'd better forget about him."

"I think so. Where are you going, Red? East?"

He shook his head, scowled.

"Then maybe the coast?"

"No." He took a deep breath. "I'm going to stay in the valley."

"In the valley?" Oldring said.

"Yes."

"How?"

"I don't know. I'll manage it somehow."

"No you won't," Oldring said bluntly. "If you stay one of Justine's men will gun you down. Maybe not the first, or the second, or even the third but sooner or later you'll run into a bullet. You can almost count on it."

"That might happen anyhow, no matter where I was."

Oldring got up. He walked to the far corner of the porch and turned and looked toward the opening to the gulch. If Justine's men were headed this way, that was the direction they would come from — and it was possible they were on their way. Watching him, Red realized that though he had not thought they would pick up his trail this quickly, he could be wrong. He got slowly to his feet.

"No one in sight, anyhow," Oldring said. "Maybe I'm just a little nervous."

"No, I shouldn't have come here," Red said. "I didn't look ahead, didn't think. I won't be by again."

Oldring scowled at him. "Don't be a damned fool. Where else would you come? I just wish I had fifty men to back me up, but I don't. If Justine rides in we'll just have to see what happens."

"I'll saddle up, anyhow," Red said. "And why don't I ride up the slope to the edge of the mesa? If I got there couldn't I see into the valley?"

"You can see for miles. That might be a good idea."

"All right, I'll do that," Red said. "Maybe we'll have time for supper."

CHAPTER
EIGHT

Ben Justine was angry. He was so angry it was hard to think. He stormed around his office, spitting out profanity, kicking at the furniture, yelling at George Adsell.

"That won't help any," George said when he could get a word in. "It's not gettin' us anywhere."

"But no trail!" Justine shouted. "No trail! How can you say there's no trail? There's got to be one. Wasn't that damned Injun out there last night, firin' at us? If it wasn't him, who was it?"

"It was him, all right."

"Then where did he go? How come he didn't leave a trail?"

"I think he was on foot," George said. "He was wearin' moccasins. That's why he didn't leave a trail."

"He had to have a horse somewhere."

"Sure, but where? He could have walked in ten miles. I don't have any idea where he might have left his horse."

"Then by God, we'll go after him. We'll search the whole damned valley if we have to. We can set up a manhunt like they never had before. We'll use every man in the valley."

120

George walked to the window. It was one of those that had been shattered by Red's bullets. George's face looked angry, but he said, mildly, "It might not be easy to set up a manhunt. Some of the men in the valley don't like us too much."

"Who cares about that?" Justine said. "The man we're after is an Injun. This was an Injun trick last night. We won't have any trouble linin' up men."

"I'd rather just go after him," George said.

"Then where would you look for him?"

"We might get a look at him at the Gallard ranch. The place is supposed to be empty, but it might not be. I think I'd look at Oldring's, that's where Myrt Gallard went. I think I'd keep an eye on Ingerhall's, an' Kreel's. Ingerhall and Kreel were close to Gallard. Once I got a glimpse of the Injun, I'd keep after him until I got him."

"Gallard's, Oldring's, Ingerhall's an' Kreel's, that's four places."

"Why not do this?" George said. "Send three men to each place?"

"That's about all the men we've got. Send two men to each place."

"All right, two to each place. But put up a reward."

"Why? To hell with that. We pay double wages as it is."

"That doesn't help Joe Stubbs."

"He took a chance. He thought he could handle the Injun."

"The men don't figure it that way any more. A reward wouldn't hurt at all. You could afford it."

121

"All right, a hundred."

"Five hundred. That's what I'll tell 'em. I've still got the five hundred I didn't pay to Rossiter, or to Stubbs."

"Five hundred, then, but I think you're puttin' up too much for a damned Injun. I wish . . ."

He broke off, whirled to the door. It had opened. Kathy was standing in the hallway, looking in. She was wearing a long, lacy, dressing gown. It was not at all revealing but to an extent it was an intimate garment and he noticed the way George's eyes had widened.

He scowled at his daughter. "What is it, Kathy?"

She looked at George, frowned, then she looked at him. "I wanted to talk to you for a minute."

He was still angry. "Go ahead and say it. What do you want?"

"I had better see you later," Kathy said.

"Better say it now, I won't be here long," Justine said. "I've got to go to town."

"Then I'll see you tonight," Kathy said. "Or next week, or next year."

She sounded mad. Maybe she was. And she turned away, disappeared from sight.

Justine glared at the empty doorway. He realized he had been too abrupt. That was one of his failings. He looked at George. "Was she frightened last night?"

"Don't think she was," George answered. "She missed most of the trouble. She didn't get in until just before you did."

"What!" Justine was shouting again, "Where had she been?"

122

"Didn't ask her," George said. "She wouldn't have told me."

Justine headed for the door. He leaned out into the hall and yelled, "Kathy! Hey, Kathy, get down here. I want to see you."

There was no answer.

He called her again, then again. There was still no answer. He moved back into the room, glared at George and after a moment he said, "Go saddle my horse. And send those men after the Injun. Tell 'em not to miss any chances. I want that Injun dead."

After George left he went upstairs, knocked on Kathy's door, then tried the handle. The door was locked.

He called, "Kathy, here I am. What was it you wanted?"

"I'll see you tonight," Kathy said. She still sounded angry.

"I'm waiting for you, Kathy."

"You better not wait," Kathy said. "George won't like it."

Justine raised his fist. He almost pounded on the door, but he didn't. Kathy was being childish and stubborn; maybe she was ready for a fight. This was not the time to talk to her.

He twisted away, went downstairs. Fifteen minutes later he and George headed for town. Eight men had been sent out on a special assignment, to take care of the Indian. Four men were to guard the ranch. He doubted that they would have any trouble. The Indian had taken a few shots at the ranch last night, but he would never get a chance to try that again. He wouldn't live that long.

George cleared his throat. "What we gonna do in town?"

"I want to talk to the sheriff," Justine said. "I want a posse sent out, after the Injun. You'll find it ain't hard to stir up a crowd if you go about it in the right way."

"Could be you're right," George said.

"I want to get this thing done," Justine said. "Then I want to run down Ed Broadwell and Frank Thompson. What the hell could have happened to them? They got to be somewhere around."

"Got to be," George said. "We'll find 'em. What about the Gallard ranch?"

"We'll run out and see Myrt Gallard, one of these days. No hurry about that. Maybe Lillian can help me with Myrt. They're good friends. I'll talk to her."

George grunted.

They reached town well before noon. The sheriff was out somewhere. Justine looked up and down the street. He could have picked out a dozen men who might as well have been out searching for the Indian. They would agree to, he thought, particularly if there was money in it.

"Might as well have a drink," George said.

"Later," Justine said. "I think I'll talk to Lillian about Myrt."

He started that way but before he had taken a step a young man stopped him. He called, "Mr. Justine, can I see you for a minute?"

124

He nodded. He was not sure who the young man was but he thought he worked for Kreel. Before very long he was going to have to have a talk with Kreel, make him a proposition.

"My name's Ed Cooper," the young man said. "I work for Kreel. I thought — I just wondered — that is, if you don't mind I'd like to call by and see your daughter, Kathy."

"Huh! Kathy!" Justine was startled. "What you want to see her for?"

It took him this long to realize what Cooper was really saying — that he was interested in Kathy, that he wanted her. He gulped and he thought, "To hell with you, Cooper. Kathy's never gonna get mixed up with a cowhand — any cowhand. Come near her an' I'll blast you . . ."

He would have liked to have said that, but he didn't. It had hit him abruptly that maybe Kathy had promoted this. She rode wherever she wanted to. She could have met him a dozen times. She might have been with him last night. He had to find out about this.

Cooper had looked away. His face had colored. He stumbled over his words. "I just kind of like her, Mr. Justine. She's a fine young woman. I've been saving my money and . . ."

"I'll think about it, Cooper," he said gruffly. "But I got some things on my mind. George!" He raised his voice. "George, buy young Cooper a drink. I'll see you both later."

Cooper nodded, but George said, gruffly, "All right Come along with me."

George Adsell was in no mood to buy a drink for Ed Cooper. If he had been Justine he would have ordered Cooper to leave the country. Or he would have done something much more drastic: he would have badgered Cooper into the position of having to go for his gun. He would have finished him.

That ought to be done, anyhow. If this was the man Kathy had been spending her time with she was making a terrible mistake. Ed Cooper had called himself a cowhand. He had drifted in from somewhere, he would drift on. He was only a saddle tramp. It was hard to understand why Kathy had liked him. Maybe she hadn't. Maybe Ed Cooper had just been hoping.

They headed for the nearest saloon, moved up to the bar and George bought the beer. He took a short drink, than he said, "Cooper, you've got good taste. Kathy's a fine girl. Know her well?"

"Pretty well," Cooper said.

"Serious about it?"

"I asked her to marry me. She hasn't said yes, but I think she will."

George grunted. "I guess you're the man she was with last night."

"We took a little ride," Cooper said.

George looked away, nodded. His face had not changed but he felt as though he was being torn apart inside. He could imagine what might have happened last night — Kathy and this man riding out somewhere. They would have come to a quiet clearing in the trees, reined up, dismounted. The man would have brought a blanket, they would have spread it out, got down on it. And after that . . .

He slammed his fist down on the bar, then he laughed to cover up the way he felt. He finished his beer, ordered a straight shot of whiskey and drank it. A plan was unfolding in his mind and he said, slowly, "Maybe you'd like to know where Kathy is, right now?"

"She said she was going to stay home today," Cooper said.

"She did, most of the mornin', but then she rode out. I know where she is. Maybe you'd like to surprise her?"

"I want to wait to see Mr. Justine," Cooper said.

"He won't be back for a couple of hours. You got plenty of time. Kathy's not fifteen minutes from here."

"I can't think where that might be."

"I'll show you," George said. "Come on. We'll get our horses."

He started toward the door but stopped, and looked back. Cooper was still there at the bar. There was a puzzled expression on his face.

"What's the matter? Ain't you goin'?" George asked.

"No, I think I'll wait right here," Cooper said. "It's rather important to me to see Mr. Justine. Thanks all the same."

George shrugged, and he headed on toward the door. "The damned fool," he was thinking. "This won't save him. An' he's never gonna see Kathy again. He won't live that long." He had some planning to do. He couldn't put it off another day. Maybe he ought to ride

127

out and not wait for Justine, who might have a job for him.

He was outside by this time and he nodded to himself and moved toward his horse. A moment later he was riding out, headed for the Justine ranch, but he wasn't going there. He would swing east. He would wait for Cooper somewhere between Dry Fork and the Kreel ranch.

Red Pardee was having a hard time. They were all against him, Myrt, Sally, Fran and Carl Oldring. Of course, they were not against him as a person. They were against his announced plan to stay in the valley. Myrt was worse than anyone else. She argued, and argued, and argued. She got angry, she begged, she almost cried. Sally said a few things, Fran agreed, and Oldring put up a good argument. Red listened to all of them.

"If you stay you don't have a plan," Oldring said.

"They'll ride you down," Myrt said. "They'll kill you."

"You can't fight them all," Sally said. "There are too many."

"I don't think you have to go east," Fran said. "But I don't see how you can stay here. What's the matter with the mountains?"

"Nothing's the matter with the mountains, I like them," Red said. "I know Justine has too many men, I might get killed and I don't have a plan. But I might find a plan, I might not get killed, and some of Justine's men might not stand by him."

"Why do you really want to stay here?" Oldring asked.

"I saw what happened to Tom Gallard," Red said. "I know what he wanted — just to be left alone. But Justine didn't leave him alone. He wouldn't leave me alone. I think I want to make Justine look at me as a person with the same rights as he has."

"You'll never get that out of Justine."

"Maybe not, but I don't have to agree with him. If I leave, that's to agree with him, to admit I'm not good enough to stay."

"Why will the rest of us have to leave?"

"You're in the way. He wants your land and property, he wants my life." Red looked away. "People fight for different reasons. Is it better to fight for money or for a name?"

Oldring scowled at Myrt. "Did you teach him to think this way?"

"I didn't have to," Myrt said. "All the arguments are on Red's side. I — I just don't want him to be hurt."

It had been a quiet night. As far as they could tell, none of Justine's men had come near them. Red had slept outside. He was fairly sure that no one had moved in during the night, the horses or the two dogs would have heard them. Then, shortly after dawn, Red had climbed to the ridge and looked out across the valley. There was no one heading this way.

"Some of Justine's men ought to ride in today," Oldring said. "I've got the feeling they will. We ought to go in hiding, Red. I want to see how the women get along without us."

"You mean, talking back to Justine?" Red asked.

"Yep. They're gonna have to. I think they'll do all right."

"I can leave any time," Red said. "I can head down the ridge and later cut into the valley."

"I want you to make it to one of those hideouts you told me about. You can't fight Justine alone."

"When will you start for Prescott?"

"Right after Justine's men show up — and leave. That ought to be today."

Red got to his feet. "I want to walk down to see my horse, Night. I've got to tell him I won't be around for a while."

"I'll go with you," Fran said.

They left the house, walked down toward the old corral. Oldring had said he had some paper work to finish, Myrt and Sally had headed toward the kitchen.

"Know what they're doing?" Fran said. "They're putting up a lunch for you. They'll both worry about you. I will too."

He was frowning. "Do you think I'm wrong to stay here?"

"No. But I don't want you to get killed."

"I don't either," Red said, and his frown vanished. "Hey, look at that horse. He knew I was coming. You can tell that by the way he's standing. Notice his eyes!"

"I want to see you ride him."

"Not today. Maybe next time. Or maybe you'll ride him first. Talk to him every day, several times. Get him used to the sound of your voice and the touch of your hand. If you take your time when you mount him he

130

won't buck — he'll just tear out like all of Justine's men were after you — and he'll run away from them."

"Do you really think I could gentle him?"

"Yes. Take your time. You can do it."

He moved up to the corral, leaned against it, and he started talking to the horse. He called, "How you feelin', Night? You tired of this corral? Maybe you'd like to tear out of here, streak down the gulch, get away? I bet you'd love it."

He started to climb the fence but stopped. Fran, just off to the side, had gasped. He heard that, but in a dim sort of way. His entire concentration had been on the horse. There had been nothing else on his mind. Suddenly there was. Fran had gasped. She had stiffened. He could sense that more than see it. She had gasped, stiffened, and now she was looking somewhere behind him. There was a shed back there, some scrubby shrubs, a couple of trees and an old wagon. And there was something else back there, something that didn't belong.

He was wearing his gun, but he was not sure he would ever be able to reach it. He could turn, but what then? What would happen? If he waited . . .

Fran took a quick, deep breath.

She started to scream.

There was no time to turn. Red threw himself back. He clawed desperately at his gun, reached it, drew it. A bullet streaked above him, and another. He heard those shots before he hit the ground. He heard two more as he rolled over and he felt a blow over the head. It was like the edge of a board, hitting him hard. Two men were back there near the shed. They must have been behind it when he and Fran walked down here but they were now in front of it.

Red fired at one of the men, then he fired at the other.

The first man seemed to disappear. Maybe he went down; but the second man didn't. He wobbled from side to side. He still had his gun and he was trying to lift it. He was a short, hunched man, one of Justine's riders. His gun was up, now, and he fired it but the bullet kicked high. Red tried to steady his own gun but that pain in his head was worse and a sudden wave of darkness swept over him. It seemed to blot out everything.

CHAPTER
NINE

Red woke up, but he didn't want to. His mind was fuzzy. It was hard to think, it was hard to remember what had happened. There was a throbbing pain in his head. It seemed hot; he was perspiring. He could hear someone talking but he couldn't make out the words. Something cool and soothing touched his face. It was like a moist cloth. He knew he ought to say something in appreciation but while he was thinking about that he fell asleep.

When he woke up again it was dark and it was cooler. He could feel that he was in a bed. His head hurt, and he remembered suddenly the brief gunfight near the old corral. "They brought me here, afterwards," he thought. "And I'm still here. That's wrong. If Justine finds me here he'll have all the excuse he needs to smash the Oldrings. I've got to get away."

A door opened. Someone moved into the room and came toward the bed. There was hardly any light but he guessed it was Myrt. He could tell by the faint smell of her clothing.

He spoke her name. "Myrt?"

She moved closer, reached down, and brushed her hand across his cheek. She said, "Yes, Red. What is it? Would you like some water?"

"No. Where am I? Still at Oldrings'?"

"Of course you are."

"But I can't stay here. You know that."

"Mr. Oldring thinks you might be able to ride in a day or two."

"That's not soon enough."

She probably smiled although he couldn't see it. She spoke quietly. "We have to be practical, Red. You were in no condition to ride today. You won't be tomorrow. The bullet grazed the bone of your skull. It almost killed you. You ought to spend the next two days resting."

"But not here," Red said.

"There's no other place to go."

"What if Justine rides in?"

"There's little chance he'll ride in tonight," Myrt said. "We can talk about what to do about Justine in the morning. Now I want you to rest, go back to sleep."

He frowned, reached up and touched his bandaged head. It still hurt pretty bad. It took an effort to think.

"Good night, Red," Myrt said.

"No, wait," he said quickly. "There were two men . . ."

"They will not bother us, ever. Now go to sleep."

"They had horses."

"Mr. Oldring took care of them. And he took care of your horse, too. He'll explain in the morning."

134

He had another question. "Is Fran all right? There was a lot of shooting and . . ."

"She's just fine, Red, but if you keep on talking you'll wake her up. She's in the next room."

"Myrt, I have to move out tomorrow," he said, definitely.

"We'll talk about it, Red," Myrt said.

She left a moment later and Red started thinking about what she had said. A head wound was not serious. Tomorrow, early . . .

He had some thinking to do, a plan to outline. He had not meant to fall asleep, but he did.

Oldring came in to see him the next morning. He had shaved and he seemed to have relaxed. He showed no signs of anxiety. He said, "Morning, Red. You look a lot better. How's the head?"

"Pounding," Red answered.

"If you take a blow like that you're supposed to feel it. But this wound won't keep you down too long. In another day we might have you on your feet."

"Or in an hour," Red said.

"No. Not that soon. Besides, you don't have a horse. I took your horse and two others, unsaddled them, and led them down the valley. Turned them loose where the water and grass are pretty good. It might be days before they're found."

"And the two men?"

"Buried. I saved their personal belongings. I'll have to report their deaths to the authorities, but I won't be able to do that for a while. I'd reckon that Justine will be wondering what happened to them. He might even get worried."

"I think one was Lou Kemp," Red said. "The other was called Lambert."

"That's right. Two men who worked for Justine. My daughter says that they didn't intend to give you a chance. She saw 'em come in sight and draw their guns. She was sure they meant to shoot. I guess she screamed."

"I threw myself back," Red said. "If she hadn't warned me . . ."

"But she did. Do you know, they came over the ridge, moved in during the night? I made sure this morning, now, that there's no one around."

"You were going to start for Prescott," Red reminded him.

"I still mean to go there," Oldring said, "but I've put off leaving for awhile. I want to see how the women handle Justine when he rides in."

"I've got to be gone before then," Red said.

"Not necessarily. Sally won't let anyone inside while I'm gone. Justine might not like it but he knows the custom. Women are left alone on the ranch quite often. They're not supposed to be bothered."

"Justine's not the average man."

"He is in a lot of ways."

"I still don't think I ought to stay."

"You don't? Then sit up. Go ahead, try it."

Red tried it. He sat up, and maybe he did it too quickly. A wave of dizziness swept over him. If he had been standing he would have fallen. Sitting in the bed he merely turned over on his side, covered his eyes. His head was suddenly pounding more. He felt sick at the stomach.

"Don't worry," Oldring said. "Just take a little more time. The wound wasn't bad. The bullet jarred your head. You're lucky you're alive."

Red took a deep breath. He wanted to get away from here but it seemed he couldn't, right now. Maybe by night he would feel better. Definitely, he would make it tomorrow.

He stretched out on the bed, his eyes still closed.

"Be in to see you later," Oldring said.

"Where's my gun?" Red asked.

"On the dresser. Want it?"

"I'll want it if Justine shows up."

"He won't be here this morning," Oldring said. "If you want anything, just yell."

He was not going to have to yell. Myrt was in to see him, then Sally, then Fran. The three women were in and out of his room all morning. After only a little time he decided that no one had ever been better cared for. All three seemed to think he ought to stay. It seemed to be their common feeling that Justine would not appear for several days, and if he did he would give them no trouble.

"If he rides in, I will talk to him," Sally said. "This is my home, and I will tell him so. And I will not invite him in."

"I will be at the window, with a rifle," Myrt said.

Fran nodded. "I'll have a rifle at the window on the other side."

"So you are not to worry," Fran said. "We just want you to get well."

From the way the three women said it, it seemed that there was no problem. Maybe they were right. It could be that Justine would back off, leave the women alone. At least in the beginning he might do that. But how about the next day, and the next and the next? And what about some of his men, George Adsell, Oily Durand, Chubby Quinn? How far could they be trusted to abide by the customs?

In the middle of the afternoon he sat up again and the dizziness came back, but it was not as bad as the first time. If he could stay here another night he might feel a lot more steady in the morning.

The day passed. Toward dusk Oldring reported that right now, at least, he could see no one headed this way across the valley. "Justine won't hit us at night. I'm pretty sure of that. We ought to have another quiet night."

Justine was pacing the room again. Nothing was working right. He had pushed up against Ed Broadwell and Frank Thompson, had pressured them to sell out. He had given them a deadline but what had happened? The two men had sent their families away, then they had disappeared. They were still missing.

Another thing — he was getting nowhere with Lillian. The last time he had talked to her she had almost closed the door in his face.

138

He had seen an end to Tom Gallard. That was one thing in his favor. But the Indian who had killed Rossiter and then Joe Stubbs, and who had dared to shoot up the ranch as a gesture of defiance, was still at large. In two days the sheriff's posse had not found him. And the men sent out by George Adsell had accomplished nothing. There was still a chance that the two men sent across the valley to Oldring's might have learned something. George had not heard from them. He was hopeful but Justine wasn't. When things started going wrong, then for a time everything went wrong.

It was morning of another day. Justine had his coffee, then he went outside. George walked toward him from the bunkhouse, and he shook his head. "They didn't ride in last night."

"Lambert and Kemp, the two men who headed toward Oldring's?"

"Yep. They're good men, too."

"Good like Joe Stubbs?"

"That was a damned accident," George said. "The Injun's been ridin' his luck. Let's ride over to Oldring's an' see what's happened."

Justine thought for a moment, then he nodded. "Good idea, but pick only four men. I don't want to seem to have too much of a crowd. You and me and four men. That's all we'd need if we was runnin' into trouble."

"Grub?"

"Naw. We'll get somethin' there. I want two men in town, two men hear Gallard's, an' two men keepin' an eye on Ingerhall. I got word that he's ready to pull out."

"That'll make it easier on us," George said.

"We'll start right after breakfast," Justine said, and he turned back toward the house, but stopped, looked back, and called, "George, come back here a minute."

George did. He had a lumbering walk. He was too heavy for his height. He said, "Yeah?"

"Whatever happened to that man who wanted to call on my daughter?" Justine asked.

"Don' know," George said, but his scowl deepened. "Ain't you been keepin' Kathy in?"

"At night. Not in the day. She was away most of yesterday."

"I didn't think about her meetin' him during the day," George said, and his hands closed, balled into two massive fists. "If I find him around here . . ."

"If you do, call me," Justine said. "I'm Kathy's father."

George grunted, nodded, and he stared off into the distance. His scowl was still there.

Justine, George Adsell and four other riders left the ranch about half an hour later. They headed across the valley, but not directly toward Oldring's. On the way they stopped by at Thompson's, then at Broadwell's. Both places were vacant. There were no signs that anyone had been there recently.

"Where could those two men have gone?" Justine muttered. "They wouldn't have just left, an' left everything behind. They've got to be somewhere around."

140

"They're layin' low," George said. "They're waitin' to see what happens."

"Sure, but where are they? Dammit, I wish I knew."

But he didn't and they rode on, this time directly toward Oldring's. A mile south of the mouth to the gulch they came to the wagon road and followed it, came to the drift fence and the gate and opened it and moved on.

"We want this place too?" George asked.

"Sure, but there's no hurry." Justine answered. "This will fall in our laps after we've cleared out this end of the valley. Oldring won't be any problem. What do you think has happened to our two men?"

"They might be hidin' out somewhere. I told them that this was where the Injun might come. I told 'em to keep under cover, to blast him down if they saw him."

"Did they take much grub?"

"I told 'em to get enough for several days. They got to be somewhere around."

They had been following the road up the gulch and now they were getting close to the ranch house. Two more minutes and they pulled up in the yard. A woman had come out on the porch. She was not a very large woman. Today she was wearing a bright blue-and-white patterned dress. She had dark, glistening hair, and she seemed to be smiling. She had always seemed neat and pleasant.

Justine touched his hat. "Nice to see you, Mrs. Oldring. Is Carl here?"

"No, he's away somewhere," the woman answered. "I'm very sorry."

"Expect him back soon?"

"He might ride in any time."

"Isn't Mrs. Gallard staying here?"

"Yes. She's here, and my daughter is here. I'm not alone, Mr. Justine."

He nodded, and he didn't know what to say next. Now that he was here he would have liked to look through the gulch, search the buildings. The Indian might be here. In fact, there was a good chance he was. Myrt was here and if she could she would be protecting him. A thought crossed his mind and he leaned forward. "Mrs. Oldring, it's been a long ride. I know it's askin' a lot, but if you could put out some food we'd sure be grateful. How about it?"

She surprised him. She shook her head. "No, Mr. Justine."

"Huh?" He couldn't believe what he had heard.

"I said, no, Mr. Justine." She shook her head. "It's not far back across the valley. I think you can make it with no trouble."

He raised his hand, pushed his hat back and he was angry. This lack of courtesy grated against him. What was the matter with this woman, anyhow? She had probably been listening to Myrt Gallard. That was the trouble.

He raised his voice. "Listen to me, Mrs. Oldring. We been ridin' hard, lookin' for the Injun. As a matter of common courtesy you could have put out some coffee, at least. At any other place . . ."

"The Indian?" Sally asked.

142

"That's what I said. The Injun. Maybe he's been here."

"If you are talking about Red Pardee, he has been here many times. He has always been welcomed."

"Could be he's there now."

"If he was, I wouldn't tell you," Sally said.

Justine was suddenly glad they had come. The Indian was here, cowering inside the house. He turned and said, "George, you an' Durand and Quinn, pile down from your horses and go in the house an' get him — the Injun."

George nodded, swung down from his horse and started toward the porch steps. Durand and Quinn dismounted and followed him.

"Stop right there!" another voice said.

A woman was standing back of one of the open windows. She was holding a rifle, pointing it at George and the two men with him. All three had stopped. Justine could see the woman clearly. It was Myrt.

"She won't try anything," he called. "Go ahead, George."

"Sure," George said. He took off his hat, smiled and said, "Sorry, Mrs. Gallard, but we got a job to do."

He took a step forward, and another.

Myrt fired the rifle. The bullet must have come close to George. He ducked, stopped abruptly, and stared wide-eyed at Myrt. The two men with him had stopped.

Justine was almost shocked. He hadn't thought Myrt would use the rifle. A sudden anger swelled up inside of him. He leaned forward and yelled, "Myrt Gallard, you put up that rifle. What has happened to you, anyhow? Put it up!"

She didn't look at him, she didn't answer him. She didn't put up the rifle. She had pumped another shell into the firing chamber and she was watching George.

She had something to say, too. She spoke very clearly. "Mr. Adsell, if you take another step toward the house I will put a bullet through your shoulder. If that is what you want, come right ahead."

"George, you go right ahead," Justine shouted. "She's just bluffin', she don't mean it. Go an' get that Injun."

"I think that you and your men better leave," Sally said. "Myrt will do what she said, and if there is any trouble, my daughter is at the other window — with a rifle. She is an expert shot."

Justine took a quick look at the other window. Mrs. Oldring had been right that her daughter was at the other window, holding a rifle. It was aimed straight at him. It ran through his mind that he could whip up his gun, drop the girl before she fired. Then he could turn his attention to Myrt, and get her too — but he hadn't counted on anything like this — a fight with two women. No, three women. Mrs. Oldring had turned away, reached to the porch swing. In the seat was a rifle. She had picked it up. From the way she handled it she knew how to use it.

He had to say something. George hadn't moved any nearer the house, and he probably wouldn't. If it came to a shootout — but he still couldn't think of a shootout with three women.

He made a gruff comment. "You're makin' a bad mistake, Mrs. Oldring. You're standin' in the way of law an' order."

"Law and order?" Sally said. "What have you got to do with law and order?"

"You're defendin' the Injun."

"Who says so?" Sally shook her head. "Let me tell you what you tried to do. You tried to search my house, without the sheriff and without a court order. What right do you have to even question me?"

"I tell you . . ."

"Don't tell me anything."

Justine glared at her. He was so mad he could hardly talk, but he pointed his finger at her and he shouted, "Woman, you're gonna be sorry about this. Damned sorry." He glanced at George and the two men near him. "Come on. Let's get out of here."

His ride back through the gulch was rather silent. So far as he was concerned, things were still going wrong.

There had been five men with him. There were five men with him as he headed back toward the valley. Oldring watched from a bedroom window then he went outside and climbed to the ridge. From there he watched Justine and the five men start across the valley.

"Don't know why some didn't stay," he told Red later. "One could have gone for help, five could have stayed here, pinned us down. Might have been they wasn't ready for anything like that — didn't have any grub, any blanket rolls. An' of course they can't be sure you're here."

"I won't be here, tomorrow," Red said.

Oldring shook his head. "I don't know. You're still shaky. What do you think of Sally, Myrt, and Fran?"

"I'm glad they're not against me."

"I think they did fine," Oldring said. "But I don't know what might happen next time. I'm kind of worried about leaving."

He scowled, and turned and left.

Red sat up. He did feel a little shaky, a little dizzy, but he knew he was better than yesterday. He got out of bed, steadied himself, walked to the window and back, and he made it but he was glad when he got back to the bed. He thought, "Tomorrow I'll make it. I can't wait any longer."

Fran came in to see him in the late afternoon, and her eyes were sparkling, she was breathing fast and there was color in her cheeks. She almost tripped over her words. "I've been down to see Night. I climbed over the fence. I — I even touched him, put my hand on his shoulder and he let me."

"Did you talk to him?"

"Just like you did. I mean, I tried to talk like you did. I think he likes me — a little."

Red laughed. "You're doing all right, Fran. But don't hurry him. Take your time. I want you to ride him, first, bareback."

"Bareback! I'm not sure I can."

"Swing on top of him, stay only a minute, then swing to the ground."

"But to get on him . . ."

Red grinned. "Go practice. Start with . . ."

146

He broke off as Oldring appeared in the doorway, and there was a curious look on his face. The man glanced at Fran, but then he said, "Two men here to see you, Red. Do you mind?"

Red looked toward the dresser, and his gun. He said, "What two men? Who . . ."

"I don't think you'll need your gun," Oldring said. "Shall I bring them in? One is Chet Ingerhall, the other is Ed Cooper."

Red was amazed. It was just about a year ago that he and Chet had their fight. It had been a rough fight. After it, Chet had declared that some day they would have another, and the next time he would kill him. Since then, Red had seen him only a few times. He had never been friendly. As for Ed Cooper, he hardly knew him. He worked for Fred Kreel, down the valley. He couldn't think why either one wanted to see him.

"What's it all about, Oldring?" Red asked.

"They'll tell you," Oldring said, and he turned away. "I'll bring them in."

"And I'd better leave," Fran said. "I'll be in later." She followed her father outside.

Red took another look at the gun on the dresser. He could have climbed out of bed and gone after it, but he decided not to. What did Chet want of him, what did the other man want? He shook his head. He could not even guess at the answer.

Oldring came back in with two young men. They were not much older than he was. Both were tall but Chet was the taller and he was heavier than a year ago.

147

Maybe he could put up a better fight. Ed Cooper was frowning.

"Hello, Red," Chet said. "Mr. Oldring said you had a close call. I'm glad it wasn't worse. I guess you know Ed Cooper."

Red nodded. "Oldring said you wanted to see me."

"We thought you might want two recruits," Chet said. "Don't know how good we are but you might use us. We both got good reasons for joining up."

"Joining up?" Red said. "Recruits? I don't think I understand."

Oldring spoke up. "Chet, tell Red what your father and mother are doing."

"They're packing up," Chet said. "They say they know what's coming. When Justine closes in, my father says, he'll make the best deal he can, then they'll leave. He says he can't buck Justine all alone, and that's the way things work out. He goes after one man, then another. If they could get together they could put up a fight, but there's no one to pull them together. My folks are ready to quit. They told me to keep out of it, but I rode out here, with Ed. He was looking for you."

"Now let's have your story, Ed," Oldring said.

"Sure, my story," Ed Cooper said. "I don't know what you'll think of it, but I sort of got to know Kathy Justine." A flush of color showed up in his face. He broke off, looked away.

"Go ahead," Oldring said. "You're young and she's young. This is the normal thing to happen."

"Kathy didn't want to run away," Cooper said. "She wanted me to talk to her father, so I did. At least I tried

148

to but he walked off, left me with George Adsell, and like a fool I told Adsell how much I like Kathy. He seemed to understand. He even wanted me to ride out with him — to a place where I would meet Kathy. But I'm sure she wasn't there. If I had gone with him I think he would have killed me. Later that day he tried, he shot at me but from quite a distance away. He missed me, but the next time he might not miss." The man cleared his throat. "I don't think I earned getting shot at, Red."

Oldring was nodding. "They want to ride with you. What do you think of that?"

Red wasn't sure what to think. A man he had fought with and a man he hardly knew had come out here to ride with him. If they did they would be riding against Justine, but that was what they wanted. He hoped they knew what that meant.

He spoke slowly. "They're after me, you know. Not only Justine, but the sheriff and some of the men from town."

"The sheriff's just backing up Justine," Chet said. "He's not very important."

"We'll be in the saddle a lot. There won't be much rest."

Cooper shrugged. "Who cares about rest."

"Chances are, we'll get run down."

"That could happen." It was Chet who said that. "We knew that when we rode out here."

Red looked away. In some way or other he was going to stand up against Justine. With two men beside him, he could do three times better. He wanted these men.

He wanted a few more, enough so that it counted. He did have two more men — maybe. He was thinking of Ed Broadwell and Frank Thompson, who had gone to Tom Gallard for advice and who had been sent to the mountains to wait.

He sat up, looked at Chet and Cooper, and he was suddenly excited. "You want to ride with me?"

Both nodded, and Cooper said, "That's why we came here."

"We might have two more," he said slowly, and he mentioned Ed Broadwell and Frank Thompson. "They went to Tom Gallard, wanted to know what to do about Justine. Gallard sent them to a place in the mountains, to wait. They might join us."

"That makes five," Chet said.

"Make it six," Oldring said. "I might as well go along."

"Seven," Myrt said, and she moved into the room. "Now don't argue with me, Red. I can handle a rifle almost as well as you can."

He scowled, but shook his head.

Sally and Fran had crowded into the room, and Oldring said, "I suppose you want to go too?"

"We surely don't intend to stay here," Sally said. "Besides, someone's got to do the cooking, look after your camp wherever it is. So make it nine — nine rebels. I'll start packing our supplies." She started to leave.

Red turned to Oldring. "You can't let her do it."

The man shook his head. "You don't know Sally. When she says she wants to do something, she does.

150

Besides, I'd rather have her riding with me, fighting back. With what's already happened, I don't think we can leave them behind."

"I guess we've got to do some planning," Chet said. "Red, I'm sure glad we found you."

Red didn't answer. He was thinking of the first part of Chet's statement. They had to do some planning. They did. And they had to do it right now, before Justine could get back with a crowd behind him.

CHAPTER
TEN

They picked out seven saddle horses, and saved them, but moved them up the gulch near the edge of the mesa, and tied them there. Oldring led the remainder of the horses down the valley to the stand of timber where he had left the three horses before, the ones Kemp and Lambert had been riding and Red's. Before he left with them he took a look into the valley from the ridge. As well as he could tell, no riders were headed here. It might be tomorrow before they heard from Justine.

Fran and Myrt had joined Sally in packaging the food. Everyone would carry two gunnysacks, tied across the saddle. That meant that if anyone got separated from the others, he would not be left without food. Extra grain and water was provided for the chickens. If they had a chance, one of them would ride by in a few days and see how the chickens were doing. Everyone was provided with a bedroll. Most had slickers. Such ammunition as they had was divided as equally as they could. They were going to have to get more ammunition; that meant that in a day two, someone was going to have to go to town.

"What about Night?" Fran asked, and she was staring at Red. "Could I — try him?"

Red shook his head. "He's not ready."

"Then — what about him?"

"We'll have to let him go," Red said bluntly.

"Oh, no."

"I don't want to let him go," Red said. "But there's nothing else to do. We can't take him with us, he would be too much of a problem. If we left him one of Justine's men would claim him and I don't want that to happen."

Fran bit her lip. "You'll never get another horse like him."

"Not exactly like him. Maybe we can find him, some day. We'll let him go on the mesa. He'll head for the mountains, I'm almost sure. There are several bands of wild horses in the lower hills. He'll get along, fine."

"When will you let him go?"

"Tonight, I think. After your father gets back. Go tell him goodbye for me."

"You ought to do that yourself."

"Maybe I can."

"No, I'll tell him," Fran said quickly. "You stay in bed."

Red dressed, then he took a short walk around the room. He thought he did rather well but he was not sure what would happen if he tried to stay in the saddle. The next day was not going to be easy.

Cooper came in just after dusk. He had been on the ridge. No one seemed to be heading this way. "But what about tonight?" he asked. "You hadn't decided what to do when I headed up to the ridge."

"We move out tonight, after supper," Red answered. "We'll camp near the mesa but two men will guard the gate. Everyone seems to think that we won't have any trouble until tomorrow."

"Then why not stay inside?"

"We're playing safe. We've got to." Red said. "Do you know what Oldring said — we could lose everything in one night, in one mistake. That's something to remember."

Cooper nodded. "You know, I hardly know him, and I never thought he amounted to much. Kreel says that Oldring is nothing but a dirt farmer."

"In a way that's what he is but when he talks, listen to him. He might not say much but what he says cuts right to the heart of the problem."

The man grinned. "I told Kreel about Kathy. He said I was a damn fool to look at her. Oldring said that was the natural thing to do. I guess you're right about him. Anything I can do right now?"

"Ask Sally or Myrt. I'm sure they're still busy."

Oldring rode in. They had supper, then Oldring and Chet Ingerhall moved down to the gate, to stand watch, and the others headed up the slope, to their first night camp. They had one other job to be handled. Night had to be led up the hill to the mesa. Fran did that, riding her own horse and leading Night. At the mesa edge she called Red, and she said, "All right, you let him go."

It had taken an extra effort to ride to the edge of the mesa, but Red made it, and now he dismounted, crossed to where Fran had stopped. He took the lead rope from her hand, turned to look at the horse. Night had turned toward the mountains. His head arched high.

"Do you know what's going to happen?" Red said "We're gonna let you go. That's right. I don't want to do this, but I've got to. I want you to head for the mountains but don't get lost — don't go too far. Some day soon, I'm going to go after you — and that's a promise. A faithful promise."

He worked his way along the lead rope, still talking. He came to Night's shoulder, slipped the rope over the horse's head, patted him on the neck. The horse stood there. He might not have known he was free.

Red raised his voice. "All right, Night, head for the hills. I'll be seeing you soon."

The horse streaked away but after only a dozen steps he stopped, whirled to look back, reared up into the air, pounded down and snorted, and there was a free sound to it, a sound of victory.

"Goodbye, Night," Fran called.

The horse snorted again, twisted away and in another moment he had disappeared in the darkness.

"We'll never see him again," Fran said.

"No, we'll see him again," Red said. "When I can, I'll go after him."

* * *

They had no trouble that night. No one came to the gulch but by midmorning Oldring reported that a number of men were headed their way, over the valley.

"How far away are they?" Red asked.

"About an hour," Oldring guessed.

"All right, it's time to leave," Red nodded. "Some of us will head down the mesa but we'll stay near the ridge, near the valley. Four of us will stay here for a time — the men."

"You ride with them," Oldring said. "You ought to take it easy another day."

"I'll take his place," Myrt said. "I'd like to."

Red hesitated, but he knew it would be wise if he left now and what he had in mind was not too dangerous, so he nodded. "All right. Sally, Fran, and I will head down the mesa. Oldring, Chet, Cooper, and Myrt will wait on the edge of the mesa, and above the ranch house. Tie your horses out of sight of the house. Wait until our visitors are in the yard, then open up with your rifles. I like horses but I'd rather shoot horses than people. If you drop four horses, then eight men have to ride double. That cuts down the pursuit. Hit them once, maybe twice, then head for your horses and get away quick. Does that sound all right?"

"Sounds all right to me," Oldring said. "I don't like to shoot people, either. If I have to, then we will, but this is a good way to begin."

"If Adsell is there, I'd like to scratch him," Cooper said. "I owe him something."

"If he's there, scratch him," Red said. He looked at Myrt. "You be careful."

Myrt nodded soberly. "If Mr. Justine is there, I'd like to scratch him, too. But I'll be careful."

Red motioned to Fran and to Sally to get started and a moment later they were on their way. Oldring, Chet, Cooper and Myrt remained behind.

There were grass, cactus, and clumps of shrubbery on the slopes of the gulch and continuing onto the mesa. It would have been hard to determine the exact edge of the mesa. Myrt chose a thorny shrub that was close to the edge. From behind it and around the side she could see into the yard. Oldring, Chet, and Cooper took other vantage points. Then, they had to wait.

The morning was warm on Myrt's shoulders. She fingered the rifle she was holding. It had been Tom Gallard's rifle, she was using it for him. She thought about him often. She would for a long time. Now and then she talked to him. She did now. She said, "Tom, I wish you could have heard just a little while ago. You would have been proud of him. He didn't say to kill anyone, but there are people who still think of him as an Indian."

She smiled and nodded and looked down into the gulch, waiting. The Oldrings had joined them, which was wonderful. Two young men had joined them. There were two older men waiting in the mountains. Maybe, in the days ahead, more people would join them.

She spoke again, "He's doing what you would have done, Tom. He thinks like you. I wish more people really knew him — maybe they will some day."

157

A buzzard circled high above her, another joined him, and in a little while there were more. She noticed them and she knew that the men who would be riding into the gulch would see them. They would probably still be wondering what the buzzards meant, when the shooting started. They would never guess that the buzzards had noticed four bodies, lying motionless, just waiting.

A group of men rode into the gulch. They followed the road to the ranch house, pulled up in the yard in front of the house. There were fifteen, or about that number. She was not exactly sure how many. She was a fair distance away from them but she could pick out the huge, black-bearded Ben Justine. The sheriff was with them, too. That was to make this trip legal. A few of the men might have come from the town. The rest worked for Justine.

Myrt looked down the rifle barrel. She aimed directly at Justine and she touched the trigger but then she thought, "Tom wouldn't have wanted me to shoot him like this, without any warning. He didn't think you should ever kill anyone, unless you had to, unless there was no way to avoid it." She altered her aim and she thought, "Maybe I can come awfully close to him, scratch him a little."

Oldring, who was off to her left, called out quietly, "Two shots, then we back off. Keep low. Don't let anyone see you. All right. Open fire."

Myrt squeezed the trigger, and she watched Justine. He grabbed at his cheek then he ducked and started yelling orders. Myrt thought: *I missed him, but at least*

I came close. She pumped the rifle, peered down into the yard. Everything was confusion. Several of the horses were down. Most of the men had dismounted. They were scrambling for cover. She aimed and fired at one of the horses that had reared into the air but she didn't wait to see the effect of her shot. She turned and crawled farther away. After a time she got up, then she hurried for her horse.

Chet was ahead of her, Cooper was right behind her. Oldring joined them last.

"We could have stayed longer, pinned them down most of the day," Cooper said.

"We did enough damage," Oldring said. "When they leave here they'll have to ride double. They won't follow us far."

"I nicked one shoulder," Chet said. "How about you, Cooper?"

"I missed," Cooper said. "Next time I'll come closer. What's next?"

"We'll talk to Red," Oldring said.

They had mounted by this time and were heading down the mesa. Myrt was frowning. She was thinking of the trouble ahead. Tom would have tried to find a shortcut; a range war could be too costly. What would Red do? She wished he was older, more seasoned. She hoped he hadn't learned to hate, but maybe he had already. Maybe she ought to talk to him; but she was not sure what she ought to say.

Oldring called over, "Have you got any idea of what Red is planning?"

She shook her head. "None. But I'm sure he's been thinking."

"I hope so," Oldring said.

That night they camped far down the mesa, and they let the fire die before it grew dark. They had a council of war.

"We're going to move back into the valley in the morning," Red said. "On the north edge of Cosgriff's land it's hilly and there are several good stands of timberland. We can camp there, maybe for several days. We'll pick a place, but someone's got to go after Frank Thompson and Ed Broadwell."

"I'll go after them," Myrt said. "I know where they will be, and I can talk to them, but how can I find our new camp?"

"I can ride to meet you," Fran said. "We can set up a meeting place."

"You two work it out," Red said. "Myrt can figure out how long it will take to reach the mountains, and come back. Set up your meeting place. While you're doing that, the rest of us will head for town. We want to get there the morning after tomorrow, early. If we make it early none of Justine's men ought to worry us. I want Chet and Cooper to buy up all the ammunition we can afford. Do you have any money?"

"Not much," Chet said.

Cooper shook his head.

"I've got money," Myrt said.

"I do too," Oldring said. "We'll work that out."

"Good," Red said, and he turned to Sally. "Did you bring the white wrapping paper I asked you to?"

She nodded. "But you never told me what you wanted it for."

"I want you to cut it into poster size, then I want you to print a message on it. I want the posters nailed up everywhere in town. You can all help, deciding what to put on the posters. We want more help, we want more people to join us. But more than anything we want Justine to learn about it. I want him to learn he's got a fight on his hands. We'll talk about the posters in just a minute. I think they're important."

Oldring chuckled. "You know, this is going to knock the town on its ear. It's going to make some people really think. What am I going to do while we're in town?"

"You and I are going to see the sheriff. We're going to tell the sheriff we don't want any trouble and there won't be any trouble if Justine stays in his own end of the valley. We're going to set up a deadline, one that he can't cross."

"He will, right away," Chet said.

"If he does, we'll have to do something about it," Red said. "Now let's talk about the posters."

Myrt left the next morning before dawn. She did not seem to be worried about the lonely trip to the mountains. She had made the trip a good many times before. And she trusted the two men she would meet. She told Fran she would try to be back by the following noon. They picked out an agreeable meeting place.

The others turned back into the valley in the midmorning, and by midafternoon they had picked out a camp. It was at the south edge of the hills but well back of the trees. It was only a few miles from Cosgriff's ranch house but they had seen no one. Oldring said, wryly, "Cosgriff would be having a fit if he knew we were camping on his range. He doesn't want trouble. He thinks he can get along with Justine. He would keep on thinking that up to the point of lending his wife to Ben Justine. I never liked him."

Red nodded. "Gallard didn't like him, either."

"What kind of deadline are we going to set up for Justine?"

"A fair deadline. Give him the west end of the valley, everything past Kiowa Creek and a line parallel to the desert, to the south."

"He'll holler he needs more."

"Should we give him more?"

"Nope. You're giving him more land than he needs. He'll still holler."

"I know that," Red said. "But we've got to start somewhere."

Sally showed up with two of the posters. All were different. One of these read:

JOIN THE
VALLEY VIGILANTES
DEFEND YOUR HOME
BEN JUSTINE DOES NOT OWN
THE WHOLE WORLD

162

The other poster read:

JOIN
THE VALLEY VIGILANTES
BE YOUR OWN MAN
FREEDOM IS WORTH
FIGHTING FOR

"Are these all right? Sally asked.

"Wonderful," Red said. "How many do you have?"

"Twenty. I can make more."

"Make as many as you can. Twenty is enough for the town but we can put a few on the roads, scatter a few everywhere. Justine's men will tear them down as fast as they can, but a good many will be read. Do you have a hammer and nails?"

"Chet said we would get nails and a hammer in town. He and Cooper want to help put them up."

"Let them," Red said.

"What if someone really wants to join us?"

Red looked at Oldring and Oldring said, "If anyone wants to join, get his name. We'll talk about him. We might even vote him in."

"Think we'll get anyone?" Red asked.

"We had better," Oldring said. "If most of the people don't back us up, we're whipped. It's been easy, so far. Wait until things get tough."

Red frowned, but nodded. He was thinking that it might not be so easy tomorrow morning, in town. There were too many people like Cosgriff, who wanted no trouble. There were too many people who would string along with a leader. It cost something to stand against the current.

Fran stayed at the camp through the night. The next noon she would meet Myrt, Frank Thompson, and Ed Broadwell, and lead them to the camp. The others left at about midnight, headed toward town.

They made good time, stopped toward dawn, had breakfast, then rode on. They made it to town just as the sun came up. Sally, Chet, and Cooper waited at the hardware store. They had money for ammunition, and for nails and a hammer. After they had finished their work in town they would meet Red and Oldring, down the road.

Red and Oldring headed for the sheriff's home. He had an office, but who knew when he would get there? Oldring knew where he lived.

When they got there, Oldring knocked on the door. He had to knock three times, but finally Dave Tanner showed up in the doorway, and he seemed startled at who was here.

"You!" he gasped. "You!" And he backed away from the door.

"We want to see you," Oldring said. "Me and Red. And don't start yelling. It won't help."

Red followed Oldring into the house. The sheriff gulped again, then he swallowed. He stared wide-eyed at Red.

His wife showed up at a side door. She was carrying a rifle but she didn't point it. She didn't know what to do, what to say.

164

"You put away that rifle, Mrs. Tanner," Oldring said. "We just want to talk to your husband. No one's going to get hurt."

She looked uncertainly at the rifle and when Oldring walked toward her she handed him the rifle. Oldring set it against the wall.

"You — you can't do a thing like this," the sheriff said. "When Justine gets here . . ."

"When he gets here, you tell him what happened," Red said. "And I want you to give him a message. Do you mind that?"

Tanner summoned up what courage he had. "I — I've got a warrant for your arrest."

"What for?" Red asked bluntly.

"For the murder of Jules Rossiter."

"That was a fair fight, and you know it. Ask any man who was in town."

"I've got witnesses who said you went for your gun first."

"Some of Justine's men?"

"It doesn't make any difference who said so. A witness is a witness."

"How about my witnesses?" Red asked.

"I didn't know you had any. I mean . . ."

"All right, we'll talk about that later," Red said. "Do you want to take my message?"

"It won't do any good."

"I'm going to tell you anyhow," Red said. "We want Ben Justine to back off, east of Kiowa Creek, and east of a line drawn south of the mouth of Kiowa Creek to the desert. That gives him a good fifth of the land in the valley — and that's enough for anyone."

The sheriff was silent for a moment, then he shook his head. "If I give that message to Justine he'll have a fit. He might even gun me down."

"He won't do that."

The sheriff shook his head. "You ain't got the right to set up any laws about Justine."

"We are doing it, anyhow," Oldring said. "We are drawing a deadline. Justine is going to have to move back of it."

"He won't do it."

"Then there'll be trouble."

The sheriff squinted at Oldring. After a moment he spoke. "You mean you're backin' this — this . . ."

"His name is Red Pardee."

"I know his name," the sheriff said gruffly. Then he asked, "Where's Myrt Gallard?"

"What do you want with her?" Oldring asked.

"I got her real son in jail."

"What!"

"He heard what happened to his old man an' he busted out of prison. Only thing to do is send him back, but I thought his mother might want to see him."

Red stepped forward. "Give me the key, Sheriff."

"Can't do that," the sheriff said. "You ought to know that. But if Myrt Gallard wants to come to town . . ."

"Give me the key."

The man raised his voice. "You know I can't do that. You know . . ."

166

"Myrt can't come to town, either," Red said. "You might want to hold her — for Justine. Give me the key."

"I told you I can't."

Red drew his gun. He said, "Oldring, look the other way. I'm going to borrow the key to the jail, even if I have to get a little rough." He centered his attention on the sheriff. "You had better hand it over."

The sheriff's wife spoke quickly. "Give it to him, Dave."

"Now!" Red said. "I'm in a hurry."

The sheriff took some keys from his pocket. "This is another mark against you," he said bluntly.

"Good," Red said. "Make up a list. Put everything on it." He turned to Oldring. "Keep the sheriff here for the next ten minutes, then head out of town. I'll probably be waiting for you."

Oldring frowned. "Are you going to bring . . ."

"Andy Gallard. You bet I am. Myrt has been looking forward to seeing him for years."

He turned to the door, moved outside, and hurried toward the jail.

CHAPTER
ELEVEN

The jail was at the eastern end of the main street, not far from where Red and the others had left their horses. They had seen hardly anyone on the street as they rode in. Red doubted that they would see many more before they left. It was still quite early.

He reached the jail. One of the keys he got from the sheriff unlocked the door to the office. He moved inside, crossed to the jail door and opened it. There were four cells in the jail itself. Only one was occupied. A tall, thin young man had been sitting on his bunk. He got up when Red appeared. He had dark hair and he was scowling.

"Andy Gallard?" Red said.

"That's what they call me." He had a quiet, pleasant voice.

"I'm Red Pardee," Red said.

"Well I'll be damned. You're the kid."

Red didn't know what to say to that. He remembered why he had come here and he said, "You want to get out of here?"

"Damned right I do." He nodded emphatically. "Where's my mother?"

"Heading back from the mountains, right now. We'll find her at camp. That's down the valley. We'll show you."

"Who is we?"

"Oldring, his wife, their daughter Fran, Chet Ingerhall and Ed Cooper. We had a few things to do in town. You'll meet them."

"Have you got a horse for me?"

Red was unlocking the cell door. He shook his head. "We didn't expect to need one."

"Mine is probably at the livery stable. We'll see. I want to pick up my gun, too, if it's in the sheriff's desk. How did you get the keys to the jail?"

"I borrowed them from the sheriff," Red said, and he grinned. "We better get moving."

"That suits me," Andy said.

He headed for the sheriff's desk, found his gun and gun belt. He belted the gun around his waist. There was a rifle rack on the wall. He moved that way, picked one out and looked back at Red. "I'm borrowing the rifle. Didn't have one."

"Didn't see anything," Red said.

They went outside, headed toward the livery stable. Red looked back down the street. There were three men in front of the saloon looking this way. There were two more in front of the general store. There were two more in front of the hardware store. At least some of the men in Dry Fork realized that something was happening.

Someone had nailed a poster on the building just ahead. Andy stopped to read it. He called, "Hey, are you responsible for this?"

Red looked at it. The poster said:

DO YOU PRIZE
LIBERTY?
IF YOU DO THEN JOIN
THE VALLEY VIGILANTES

He nodded to Andy. "Yes, you can blame it on us. We had to call ourselves something."

"Reckon I can join?"

"Why not?"

Andy pushed back his hat. "You know, it's funny. When I first heard about you, I hated you. I felt like it was an insult that my father should bring in a halfbreed Indian to take my place. I even thought about busting out, to take care of you. I guess I felt partly that way, up to now. Think we can get along, you and me."

"We can try," Red said. "You better get your horse."

"Sure. Right away," Andy said.

Oldring was waiting for them in town. They rode out, and with no trouble at all. Sally, Chet, and Cooper had pulled up down the road. The two men had loaded up with ammunition. Sally, herself, had put up twenty posters. Chet and Cooper had put up a few more. Cooper had talked to several men about joining them. No one had been ready to say yes but he thought some of them would think about it.

Oldring had met Andy in town. Sally, Chet and Cooper met him down the road, and Cooper said, "If you're anything like your father, we sure need you."

170

"I've been in prison," Andy said bluntly. "That's no recommendation. They'll pick me up again but before they do, I'd like to help."

"I'm glad you're here — for Myrt," Sally said. "She needs you. Red, I hope you don't mind how I feel."

"That's all right," Red said. "I'm the one who borrowed the keys to the jail. I wonder how Justine will feel when he rides in."

"He'll have a stroke," Sally said.

"No, he won't do that," Chet said. "But he'll start yelling. He's not going to like us at all."

"He'll have a posse out by noon," Oldring said. "We're going to have to start running."

"Not yet," Red said. "We'll have another talk when we get back to camp."

He was looking ahead, or trying to. And he was wondering, what Gallard would have tried. He knew the way Gallard thought, he remembered a lot of the things he had said. Gallard had told him again and again, "Never back away from a fight. Move in closer. Start pushing, start pressing. Get the other man to back off. Keep him backing off and you get him off balance. That's a good rule in any fight. If you can't move ahead you shouldn't be fighting."

Then, another time, Gallard had said . . .

It was a long way back to the camp. He had a lot of time to think.

Ben Justine stormed around the sheriff's office. He had already done some yelling. He would do more. He was almost too angry to talk. The Indian had been here this morning. Oldring had been with him. Mrs. Oldring had been in town, too. Young Chet Ingerhall had been with her and another young man, Ed Cooper, the one who had wanted to call on Kathy. Cooper, of course, amounted to nothing. He was going to talk to Mike Ingerhall about his son. As for the Oldrings, to hell with them. They were finished already — on the run.

"You had your hands on the Injun, an' you let him go," he grated. "What kind of a sheriff are you?"

"I didn't have my hands on him," Tanner replied. "I was lookin' down Oldring's gun."

"You gave up the jail keys."

"No, he took 'em."

"We might as well not have a sheriff," Justine said. "You're not worth a damn."

He moved to the street door, looked outside. When he rode in a few minutes ago the town had been plastered with silly posters. They were all about freedom and liberty and about joining the Valley Vigilantes — and to hell with them. By this time his men should have torn down most of the posters. A good many men might have read them but if they had good sense they wouldn't join any bunch of outlaws. That's what they were — outlaws. Not vigilantes.

He turned to look back at the sheriff. "What did they come here for? They couldn't have known about Andy Gallard."

"They — wanted me to give you a message," the sheriff said.

"What message?"

"They wanted me to tell you that you had to stay back of Kiowa Creek, and a line south from there to the desert. Oldring called it a deadline. He said . . ."

"What!" Justine was yelling this time. "To hell with them!"

"I'm just tellin' you what they wanted me to . . ."

"An' to hell with you, too," Justine said, and he pounded outside.

He took a dozen deep breaths. He calmed down a little. Something was driving him toward his horse. He could call his men together. He had seven with him. He might be able to raise a few more in town. The thing to do, then, was to tear after the Indian, ride him down. He had left here three hours earlier but they could still keep after him. Maybe by night . . .

He shook his head. He was being too hasty, too impulsive. It would be better to work out a definite plan — get fifty men if he had to, start them at the west end of the valley and let them sweep to the east. Keep them moving that way until they sighted the Indian's crowd — then pour after him and never stop. Do the job right. It might cost him something, but what was money at a time like this?

He looked back into the sheriff's office. "Get up a posse for tomorrow morning, early. Each man is to carry a blanket roll and his grub. We're gonna go after the Injun, an' we're gonna keep after him until we get him."

"Might not be easy to get up a posse," Tanner said.

"Why not?"

"Most men got their own work to do."

"This is more important," Justine said. "I'll tell you what I'll do. Ten dollars, extra, above the posse fee, to everyone who's ready to go after the Injun. How about that?"

"The ten dollars might help," the sheriff said.

"It sure better," Justine said. "It sure better or you're finished — and that's a promise."

He swung away, started down the street, but stopped. Kathy was riding into town. She had been told to stay home.

He walked out into the street, waited until she reached him, then he asked, "What you doing here in town? I thought I told you to stay home."

She had the nerve to smile at him. "I didn't want to stay home."

"Maybe you expected to run into young Ed Cooper," Justine said. "You won't. He's ridin' with the Injun."

All the time he was saying that, he knew he was saying the wrong thing, but he got started, and didn't stop.

Kathy was still smiling. "I thought he might do that. I'm not surprised. George tried to kill him."

"Huh!" He was startled, shocked. "What do you mean?"

"Go ask George," Kathy said. "Then why don't you fire him? I don't see how you can stand him."

She shook out the reins, rode on past him, turned in to the tie-rail in front of Ella's dressmaking shop. She dismounted, tied her horse, and went inside. This was quite a respectable place. He could be glad that this was her destination — if it was? But what had she

174

meant about George? She didn't like him, he knew, but to accuse him of trying to kill Ed Cooper — that was going too far.

He thought, "I've got to see George, and ask him. I'll do that but there's no rush about it." He moved on down the street. He was on his way to see Lillian.

When Bill Adams had gone to bed with a bad cold about a year ago Lillian had not been worried. Bill was a man who had struggled with a bad, hacking cough for a dozen years, and he was constantly fighting off a cold. He had done pretty well, or at least she thought he had. He usually paid little attention to his colds. He ignored the persistent cough. In a few days he would probably be on his feet again.

This time, however, things didn't work out that way. Bill stayed in bed. He tried to get up. He did. But he went back to bed again. The cold hung on. The cough got worse. It took Bill more than a month to realize that he was suffering from consumption, and if he wanted to go on living he had better stay in bed. It took Lillian longer than that to realize what she faced in the years ahead. Bill would not live very long, no matter what he did. And as long as he was around he would be chiefly a problem, a man to be cared for, to be looked after. They owned this house, they owned a business, they had little money. It was comforting to know about the business but it wouldn't run itself.

A number of people encouraged Lillian to take over the business and run it herself. Tom Gallard had been one of them. He had scoffed at her fears. Whoever had said that this was a man's world didn't know what he was talking about. Go ahead and do whatever is necessary. If she was not as strong as she should have been, set up some pulleys to lighten the work. Use carts to handle heavy loads. Figure out a new life for herself.

Lillian tried it and after a few weeks she decided she liked running the store. She made a few mistakes but none were serious. Most of her business was with men, but in general they were helpful. A few would have been more than friendly but she let such men find out that she was not interested. She had a husband, she did not care for a lover. At least, that was her attitude.

Actually, only one man really bothered her. That was Ben Justine. He was a valued customer. She could not afford to lose his business, but almost any day, she might. He wanted her and he didn't care that she had a husband. He had become demanding. He had almost been rough. And the worst thing of all was something that she had admitted to herself only a few hours ago. She did not mind his attention. She would not even mind it if he got a little rough with her. There was something about him that appealed to her. It was wholly physical, she knew. The way she felt about him might even have been sinful. When she thought about him taking her in his arms her face would burn, but she had started indulging herself to an extent. She would think about him and about what he might do; then she would feel guilty and angry with herself and she would

176

remind herself that she was a respectable woman of thirty-nine — and a married woman.

She felt good today. She was smiling as she swept out the back room. No one had ever had a cleaner feed store, she was sure, and she was proud of that. There was a bell on the front door. It tinkled. That meant a customer had come in. She leaned her broom against the wall and went to see who it was, and her heart jumped when she entered the front room. Her face might even have colored but she kept her voice steady. "Hello, Ben."

"You could have rushed over to see me," Justine said.

"I never do that to a customer," she answered.

"But I'm not a customer." He walked toward her. "Anybody in the back room?"

She shook her head. "No, but I . . ."

"I want to pick out some new seed corn," he said, and he moved on, reached her and turned her around toward the door to the back room.

One of his hands had touched her breast, but lightly. Now it was firmly on her shoulder. She was thinking, "I know what he's going to do the minute we get in the back room. He'll take me in his arms and . . ."

That was happening. They were in the back room, off to the side. His arms were tightly around her, his mouth was wet against hers and she could feel his beard scratching her chin.

She hardly thought of that. Maybe she thought of nothing but she was aware of the full length of his body, pushing up against her firmly, against her legs, her stomach, her breasts. Her arms were even around him.

Her mouth had opened. It was a long time since she had been kissed like this.

Finally she pushed him away a little and she said, "No, no, no Ben. This is wrong. It's terribly wrong."

"There's nothing wrong about it," Justine said. "Only trouble is, there's no place to lie down except on the floor."

"Someone might come in," she said quickly.

"Then I'll go lock the door," Justine said, and he turned away, headed toward the front room and the front door.

Lillian was thinking, "No. I can't let him do this. I can't. Some way I've got to stop him. Some way . . ."

She wouldn't be able to stop him, she knew. She might not even try. Afterwards she would hate herself. Afterwards . . . She would think about that later.

Even before he got back from locking the door she had started loosening her clothes . . .

Myrt was off somewhere, with Andy. Red would never forget the way her face had changed when she saw her son. It really came to life. Her eyes had brightened, and the inarticulate cry that came from her throat must have startled even the birds. Red was afraid that he was already a little jealous.

"I think it was wonderful of you to bring Andy," Fran said.

Red shook his head. "There wasn't anything else to do. Besides, he adds one more to the crowd."

"You didn't even think of that."

178

"Sure I did. We could use more men. We're going to do what Tom Gallard would have done — we're going to keep the pressure on."

"How?"

"I'll tell you when Myrt and Andy get back and when we can all talk it over. We can do one of two things. We can wait for Justine's men to show up and then start running. As another choice we can split into several small groups, and start picking on the enemy. That's what we'll do — I hope."

"Are you going to leave me in a camp somewhere?"

"Don't you want to?"

"No."

He looked at her and grinned. "I won't keep you in camp."

He didn't mind her at all. In fact, he rather liked her. It was easy to talk to her. She was honest in her opinions. She didn't take an attitude before thinking about it. Sometimes she agreed with him, at times she took the other side. He used to think of her as plain, unattractive and awkward. Why he had ever thought that he was not sure. Or maybe she had changed. Her eyes had brightened, new color had come into her cheeks. It could be she was growing up.

Myrt and Andy came back, they had an early supper, then they got together and talked. They did some arguing, too. There seemed to be a lot of opinions. Oldring said that was healthy, but "In the end, we'll do what Red says. He hasn't made any mistakes yet."

Red scowled. "We can't afford any, yet we've got to take chances. That means sometimes we won't win and in the end, we might lose."

"What kind of talk is that?" Thompson muttered.

"Honest talk," Red said. "Before tomorrow night, every one of us might get killed. Or four of us might get killed. Or two. Or one. I think you ought to think about it."

"I've thought about it," Oldring said, and he looked at Sally. "If it happens, then it'll happen. What do you want me to do, Red?"

"I think we ought to move our camp tonight," Red said. "Before morning I want to get to the river, west of Justine's ranch. That means we ought to start riding soon. By morning, by the time it's light, I want three of you watching the town, Oldring, Myrt and Thompson. The rest of us, in two groups, will keep an eye on the Justine ranch. If all of Justine's men ride out, then we'll move in."

"What do we do then?" Andy asked.

"And what do we do about town?" It was Oldring who asked that.

"We'll talk about it while we ride," Red answered. "We've got most of the night to figure things out. We've got to get Justine on the defensive. Think about what we can do."

The next morning, early, Justine and eight of his men headed for town. They would join the posse in Dry Fork and would head out into the valley. Word had been received that the Indian and those with him had

180

been seen near the Cosgriff ranch. That was the direction the posse would take.

Toward midmorning, Art Fullmer and Sam Balke, who worked for Justine and who had been left at the ranch with two other men, to serve as guards, decided to take a chance on heading for town. The Indian was nowhere near. They were sure of that, so why did they need four guards at the ranch?

They were about three miles down the road and they rounded the shoulder of a hill — and ran into four armed men who had been waiting. No, there were three armed men and one woman, Sally Oldring. Two of the men were Chet Ingerhall and Ed Cooper. The third man they didn't know but what he said was definite.

"You've got two choices," Andy said. "You can get shot right here, or you can ride out, unarmed, and under promise never to come back. What'll it be?"

"Now look here . . ." Fullmer started.

"You've got about ten seconds to decide," Andy said, and he steadied his gun.

"I guess we'll ride out," Fullmer said.

"Then we'll take your guns," Andy said. "After that, slant to the south road, and keep going. Some of us will follow you — maybe most of the day. Start back and you'll run into a bullet."

"Justine owes us money," Balke said.

"Then write him a letter," Andy replied.

The two men handed over their guns. They headed toward the south road. They reached it and kept riding. There was a good reason to do that. Chet Ingerhall and

Ed Cooper had trailed behind them. Before long Fullmer and Balke had decided not to come back. How could they have explained why they had left the ranch? It was better to look for another job, somewhere else.

When Fullmer and Balke had started toward town they'd left the other two guards, Joe Wilson and Lou Cassidy, in the bunkhouse. Wilson was getting up into the late forties. He had slowed down quite a bit. He was bothered by arthritic pains. He hated to get up in the morning. If he could sit most of the day, he loved it. Lou Cassidy was almost as old as Joe Wilson, and he was lazier. Both enjoyed their present assignment. They had nothing to do but spend the time, and a nice way to spend it was playing pinochle.

They were playing at the table in the bunkhouse and were deep in the game when Red showed up in the doorway. His gun was in his hand. He didn't say anything. He didn't have to.

Cassidy gulped. He shook his head. "You ain't here. You can't be. They — they said you was down the valley."

"That was yesterday," Red said. "Do you want to pack up, get on your horses and head out?"

"I don't want to go anywhere," Cassidy said.

"Then would you like me to smash your hand, break it so you can't use it, ever? How long do you think Justine would keep you on the payroll?"

Cassidy swallowed. He looked at his hands then he looked at Joe Wilson.

182

"He could do it," Wilson said. "I saw that happen once. It's bad as not having hands. I reckon we better ride."

"Me too," Cassidy said.

"Ed Broadwell will ride you down the road, west," Red said. "Leave your guns behind. If you give Broadwell any trouble . . ."

"We won't give him any trouble," Cassidy said. "It's time to ride anyhow — while we got a chance."

There were four servants at the ranch: a Mexican stableman, two Mexican women who worked as house servants, and a Chinese cook. He was thin and old. Kathy was in her room but she stayed there with the door locked.

Red talked to the stableman, who got busy hitching a team to a wagon. In about half an hour the three Mexicans and the Chinese cook were ready to start off — across the valley and to the north. They didn't argue about leaving.

After Justine and his men and a small town posse had headed down the valley, in the direction of the Cosgriff ranch, Oldring, Myrt and Frank Thompson rode into town. Oldring and Thompson talked to as many men as would listen. Myrt spent her time with the women. Toward noon the three people met for dinner in the town's one restaurant. They compared notes. All three had found it necessary to spend considerable time defending Red Pardee. He was part Indian. A good many people didn't like that. In the last analysis, however, the real problem they faced was something else. It was an attitude, a way of looking at things. Oldring put it in words as expressed by Charlie Eckerman, the banker. There was trouble ahead. He didn't want to be mixed up in it. He didn't want to take sides. He wanted to shut his eyes and wait until the trouble went away.

"What do we do about people like that?" Thompson asked.

Myrt shook her head. "I don't know. Tom used to say . . ." She broke off, hesitated.

"What were you going to say," Oldring asked.

"Tom said this," Myrt answered. "He said, 'Push them into it — push them into the water, they'll either sink, or they'll try to swim. If they try to swim, help them.'"

"But how do we push this town into the water?" Oldring asked.

"Bring the fight here," Myrt said. "But don't ask me how to do that."

Oldring was silent for a moment, then he looked at his watch. "We'll take two more hours here. The posse won't get back sooner than that. Talk to as many people as you can. Say again and again that if Justine will stay back of the Kiowa Creek line, there will be no more fighting."

Thompson frowned. "What if the posse gets in early?"

"Keep close, to your horse. I mean to. And I want you to do that too, Myrt."

184

"I want to see Lillian Adams, this afternoon," Myrt said.

Oldring scowled. "You've heard about . . ."

"The rumor about Lillian and Ben Justine? I've heard about it. Lillian might have some influence on the man. I hope she does. Shall I go back to work?"

"Time for all of us to get busy," Oldring said.

Far down the valley the posse found nothing, not even a good trail to follow. They should have moved farther north, or they should have turned back home.

CHAPTER
TWELVE

Red called another meeting late that night. It was held after everyone got back to their new camp, north and west of the Justine ranch and in the shelter of the trees bordering the river. Everyone was tired but it had been a good day for them. Four of Justine's men had left the valley. They might ride back, but that was doubtful. In addition, four of Justine's servants were gone, and that would be annoying. Myrt, Oldring, and Frank Thompson had spent most of the day, openly, in the streets of the town. They had talked to a good many people, explained that they just wanted to be left alone. If Justine would stay back of Kiowa Creek there would be no more trouble.

"Everyone listened," Myrt said. "Privately, I think they agreed with us, but I doubt if anyone will back us up against Ben Justine. It is easier to go along with him."

"I should have headed for Prescott, talked to the governor," Oldring said.

"I heard that Justine and the governor are good friends," Broadwell said.

"But I know him, too," Oldring said. "I think he might have listened. I could still head for Prescott."

186

"We need you here," Myrt said. "Besides, we haven't done everything here that we can. Lillian might be able to help us with Justine. I didn't get to see her today."

"What could she do?" Thompson muttered.

Myrt shrugged. "Maybe nothing, but I think we should try everything we can think of. Kathy might help us."

"I can talk to her," Cooper said, "but from what she told me her father never listens to her. I'd — I'd like to see her again if I get the chance."

"What do we do tomorrow?" Andy asked. "Justine has been cut down to eight men. We could stand up against a crowd like that."

"Add the sheriff, an' the men they hired to ride on the posse," Broadwell said. "He could still count ten to fifteen men."

"There's only eight left to the ranch, nine with Justine."

Red shook his head. "Too many. We don't want to lose anyone."

"Then what do we do in the morning?"

Red turned to look at Myrt. "You really want to see this woman in town?"

"Lillian Adams? Yes I do." She nodded. "I tried to see her today but she had closed the store. Her husband might be worse, he's quite ill. I didn't have the chance to get to her house."

"I'll take you in tomorrow," Oldring said, "But we'll have to be sure the sheriff's gone, and that Justine's not in town."

"How about making it early," Red said. "I know you're tired but . . ."

"I'm not tired," Myrt said quickly. "We can leave here in time to get to town by sunup. Is that all right, Carl?"

"Sure. Get some rest. I'll wake you up when it's time to start."

Thompson spoke up. "I'll go with you."

"Now, how about the rest of us?" Cooper said.

Red spoke slowly. "I want four of you watching the town road just below Justine's ranch. Stop any single rider, or any two riders. If there are more than two riders, let them go. If you stop anyone, disarm them and give them a chance to leave the valley."

"The next men might not leave," Andy said.

"Try it once more," Red said. "Next time we'll try something else. Broadwell, you and I and Fran will keep an eye on the Justine ranch, starting at dawn. What we do depends on what Justine does."

He scowled, stared out into the darkness. He was trying to keep Justine under pressure but he was afraid that his plans for tomorrow would not be very successful. From now on, most likely, Justine would keep his men together. If he did that, eight men and himself was a striking force. He might be able to add a few more in town, build it up to a dozen men. That many men was a crowd to worry about.

The camp settled down, but not entirely. Oldring was sitting up. He was acting as guard. He had said he would rest the next night. Ed Cooper was sitting up,

188

maybe thinking about Kathy. Myrt and Andy were still up, talking in low tones. And Red was still awake. He closed his eyes, dozed, then someone touched his shoulder and woke him up and he asked, "What is it?"

"Time to get underway," Oldring said. "It's almost three."

It seemed he had hardly closed his eyes but he got up, stretched, moved down to the river and bathed his face.

Andy joined him, then he asked, bluntly, "Why don't I get to ride with Myrt?"

"For the same reason that Oldring is separated from his wife and his daughter. Each is more independent alone."

"Who gave you that idea?"

"Your father, Tom Gallard. He told me once never to send two friends on an important job. Instead, I should use two strangers, they might prod each other on. The two friends might be too careful of each other."

"I still don't want anything to happen to Myrt."

"Neither do I, Andy."

The man looked away. "You got Rossiter, the man who killed my father. But it was Justine who hired the man to do the job — so I get Justine."

"If it works out that way."

"It better." He was still scowling. "You gonna stay around here afterwards?"

"I don't know."

"I won't get to stay," Andy said. "They'll throw me back in prison so you better hang around."

"I might be able to," Red said.

Oldring, Frank Thompson, and Myrt left first. They had the longest trip — all the way to town. They wanted to get there before dawn, move in before anyone could notice them.

Andy, Chet, Cooper, and Sally Oldring moved out next. They would head for the road below the ranch. Most likely they would settle down near the place where they had stopped two of Justine's men yesterday.

Red, Fran, and Ed Broadwell had an easier ride than the others. They would move to a vantage point, north and west of the ranch. There were some timbered hills in that part of the valley. They would stop and wait on a side hill, in the shelter of the trees.

They got there in good time, dismounted, tied their horses and found a place to sit down. Fran leaned back against a tree, Red sat nearby, cross-legged, Ed Broadwell spread out his bedroll and stretched out on it.

"Don't worry about me," he said gruffly. "I won't be sleepin'."

"It won't be light for an hour," Red said. "Take it easy. Do you want to lie down, Fran?"

She shook her head. "I won't go back to sleep. Why don't you lie down?"

"I was thinking about Night," Red answered.

"I'll bet he misses us."

"Not him," Red said. "He'll never want to see us again — but he will. I'm going after him."

"You really mean that, don't you?"

190

"Yes, I really do. There might be a dozen better horses in this part of the country but I doubt it. He would be fast, and tough. He would have a lot of endurance. I've got to go after him."

"Wish I could go with you," Fran said.

"Do you like the mountains?"

"I could live there forever, but I don't suppose I'll be able to. If I were a man . . ."

"You do pretty well — for a girl."

"I ought to throw something at you," Fran said. "Say that again and I will."

They went on talking as it gradually got lighter in the eastern sky. The shadows faded. Red got up. He peered down at the distant ranch buildings. As yet, it seemed that no one was up. At least he could see no signs of it. There was no smoke lifting from the chimneytops. No one had come outside to cross to the outhouse. It occurred to him that maybe Justine didn't know his servants were gone. Maybe he was accustomed to the sound of someone getting breakfast. If he waited for that he was going to have to wait a long time.

"No one up, yet, Fran," he said, still peering at the ranch.

The girl looked up at the sky. "We're always up by this time. It's become a habit. Doesn't everyone get up early?"

Red nodded, and he asked, "What do you think, Broadwell? There's no one up."

The man must have been dozing. He opened his eyes, looked at the sky, got to his feet and peered down at the ranch buildings. After a moment he shook his head, scowling.

"I can't see anyone, either," Fran said. She was standing near Red, looking past his shoulder. "Could be there's no one here. Justine and his men could have stayed in town."

"Bet that's what happened," Broadwell said. "Or it could be that Justine an' his men joined the posse an' headed out in the valley an' never got back to town."

"No, they got back to town," Red said. "Oldring, Thompson and Myrt left town just before the posse rode in. I think Justine would have headed out here, but he didn't have to stay here. I should have had someone watching the ranch last night."

"We ain't got enough men to do everything," Thompson said.

"Maybe not," Red said. "But we should have had a man here."

He stared down at the buildings and wondered what he ought to do. If no one was here, if Justine and his men had spent the night in town, then Oldring, Myrt and Thompson were riding into trouble, into a trap. Actually, there were three possibilities. One, that Justine and his men were in town. Two, that he and his men were here but were slow getting up. Three, that they were here, but were being very quiet about it, waiting for someone to ride in and get shot. That could happen very easily. The ranch could seem deserted. He could ride in, and when he got close . . .

192

He shook his head, continued staring at the buildings. The sky was getting lighter. Before very long the sun would be climbing over the horizon.

"Well, what we gonna do?" Broadwell asked.

"I don't know yet," Red said, scowling.

"Maybe one man will sleep late," Broadwell said. "Or two or three might sleep after sunup. But not nine men an' there ought to be nine men there. An' a girl, Kathy Justine. She might be there, still asleep, but not the men. They ain't here. They either left afore we got here or they stayed in town last night."

"I think he's right," Fran said. "The men aren't here. I'm not sure about Kathy."

"We could pick her up," Broadwell said. "Myrt wanted to talk to her. Besides, it might be a good idea to keep her with us. Justine won't like it a bit."

"I'm still thinking about Oldring, Myrt, and Frank Thompson," Red said, and he kept watching the ranch buildings. "They headed for town, planned to get there about dawn. I might be wrong but I think Lillian Adams lives almost in the middle of town. That's where they were going, and if they run into Justine . . ."

Broadwell shook his head. "There might not be any trouble. What about Kathy?"

"Want to ride in and get her?"

"Why not? It wouldn't take long."

"Suppose Justine is there? Suppose some of his men are there — just waiting for someone to ride in. We did yesterday. They might think we'll try again."

Broadwell turned to stare at the ranch buildings. He was scowling.

"Want to risk it?" Red asked. "Want to ride in and see what happens?"

"No, I guess I don't," Broadwell said. "I'd rather wait until someone comes outside. Or until we're sure the place is empty."

"We won't try that, either," Red said. "We'll circle around to the road, pick up Andy, Chet, Cooper and Sally, then head for town. We might be needed there."

Oldring, Thompson and Myrt came in sight of the town as it started to grow light. Oldring had hoped to get there a little earlier, while it was still dark, but he shrugged and said to Thompson, "This ought to be all right. Not many folks get up this early."

"No one bothered us yesterday," Thompson said. "Why should we worry today?"

"The sheriff ought to be back, and his posse. You know that."

"They were after Red. Don't think they'll go after us."

"I hope you're right," Oldring said, and he turned to Myrt. "This too early for you?"

"Lillian won't be up," Myrt said. "But I can waken her. I don't think she'll mind."

"Do you really think it's going to help to talk to her?"

"It might not, or it might," Myrt was frowning. "Maybe this is a horrible thing to talk about, but Bill Adams is dying and Lillian knows it. She's known it for months. She's had time to look ahead, think about what to do. And she's been thinking about Ben Justine.

194

His wife just died. Maybe she could move in and take her place — and why not. It would be better for her than to have to depend on the feed store."

"Yes," Oldring said slowly. "But do you think Justine would listen to a woman?"

"Lillian can be a stubborn woman, and I think Justine likes her."

They were at the outskirts of the town, and they rode on, came to the main street and turned down it. The Adams' lived in a small house that was almost at the edge of the business district. It was set back from the street. There was a lawn in front and two large trees, and a barn, a shed and an outhouse behind it. The picket fence on both sides of the house was old and needed paint. So did the house.

"We'll go through the gate and cut to the back yard," Oldring said. "You can get off in front, Myrt. I'll look after your horse."

"Thanks," Myrt said. "I'll have Lillian make some coffee."

They turned in the yard, pulled up briefly until Myrt could dismount, then Oldring and Thompson circled to the back of the house, Oldring leading Myrt's horse.

They dismounted near the barn, tied their horses. There was a bench near the back door where there was a wash stand and basin. The well was off to the side. Oldring headed for the bench, Thompson walked toward the well. He lowered the bucket, drew it up, had a drink then took a tin cup from near the well and carried it to Oldring.

Oldring tried it, but he shook his head. "Not as good as a spring. How's the water at your place?"

"My place?" Thompson said. "If I can ever use it. Justine won't ever pull back of the Kiowa."

"Bet he does," Oldring said. "If we could get the whole valley stirred up . . ."

"We can't even stir up the town."

"We might, before we get through. Give us a little more time. In another week or so . . ."

Oldring broke off. He jerked a look toward the back corner of the house. A man had been there but he was gone. He had come past the building and he risked a look into the back yard, then he jerked back. Oldring caught only a glimpse of a part of his body. He had no idea who the man was.

He said, "Hey, someone was there at the corner of the house for a minute. I wonder . . ."

He got quickly to his feet, hurried to the place where the man had disappeared. There was no one in sight in the street, but it was not far to the building on the nest lot. The man must have had time to reach it and get a few steps beyond.

Thompson hurried up behind. "Did you see him? Who do you think it was?"

"I don't know who it was," Oldring said. "And I don't like this. Where did the man go? What was the hurry?"

"Why would he be looking back here, anyhow?"

"Maybe he saw us ride in. Maybe he wasn't sure who we were, so he went to take a look. But why? What for? If I thought any of Justine's men were in town . . ."

196

"They wouldn't be here this early."

"Shouldn't be, but I still don't like this, Thompson." Oldring motioned. "You get over there to the horses. Untie them. Get them ready so we can move out of here. I'm going in to get Myrt."

He headed for the back door. Thompson moved toward the barn and their horses.

Oldring had to knock on the back door several times before anyone answered. Finally, it was Myrt who answered, opened the door. She was frowning.

"Someone noticed us," Oldring said. "Don't know who it was but he scooted away. I think we had better get away from here, while we can."

Myrt bit her lips. "You mean . . ."

"I think we better run."

"Give me just one minute," Myrt said. "Go get the horses. I'll be right with you."

She turned back inside but left the door open.

Oldring swung away. He hurried toward the barn. Thompson had untied the three horses. He was holding their reins but he was looking past Oldring and to the side, and he called out, "Three of 'em headed this way. One of 'em is George Adsell. The other two . . ."

Oldring turned. He looked past the corner of the house and toward the street. From where he was standing now he could see the building on the next lot and part of the street. Three men on foot had turned the corner of the building, were headed this way. The side fence was low enough so it was no obstacle. The men stepped over it. One was George Adsell. The other two were Chubby Quinn and Erv Stafford. All three were riders for Justine.

It ran through Oldring's mind that Justine's men should not have been here. But they were. And he realized that they would get here before Myrt could get outside or mount her horse. She might make it if she showed up right now, but the three men were close enough to shoot them down. Right now, maybe, he and Thompson could race away — but what about Myrt? She could never make it.

He spoke quickly. "Pile on your horse and get out of here, Thompson. Hug the saddle and keep moving."

"But Myrt . . ."

"I'll look after her. Tell Red not to worry about us. Tell him — goddammit, start riding."

Thompson hesitated, but for only a moment. The three men were almost here. They had already drawn their handguns. He might even catch a bullet unless . . .

He swung into the saddle but he didn't go all the way. His top leg hung over the saddle, the other was braced in the stirrup. He hugged the side of the horse, the side away from the three men. Several shots screamed past him. That was about all. In another moment he would straighten in the saddle and not worry about the men behind. He would be well on his way out of town.

Oldring watched as Thompson broke away, and he thought: "Good! He's made it He'll get word to the others what happened."

He was not sure that would mean anything to him. It might be important to Myrt, but he was not sure of that either. He suddenly was not sure of anything. The three Justine hands had made it to the back yard. They had fired several shots at Thompson; now they were facing him, and they had fanned out so that they were about two yards apart. In a way, this was amusing. He was no gunfighter. He was no danger to them. They were the experts, the ones who rated the speed of their draw. He wasn't in the same class. If he even got a chance to reach his gun . . .

George Adsell barked a question. "Where's the Injun — inside?"

Oldring moistened his lips. "You mean Red Pardee?"

"Red Pardee? The Injun. Where is he?"

"Up the valley," Oldring said. "Or maybe he's down the valley. It's hard to keep track of him."

"I think you're lyin'," George said. "Erv, keep an eye on him. Me an' Chubby will look inside the house."

Erv Stafford shook his head. "You might need me with the Injun. This is the way to take care of Oldring."

The man was holding his gun. Now he raised it, slowly, deliberately. There was a tight, ugly smile on his lips. His eyes had narrowed until they were nothing but slits.

Oldring knew what was going to happen. He had sensed the possibilities the moment he saw them running this way. He should have been prepared for this but he wasn't. He started to cry out. He grabbed for his gun but just as he reached it something hit him hard in the shoulder.

He staggered back, fell, and as he crashed into the ground he thought he heard another shot, but he was not sure about that and there was not time to wonder about it.

Myrt Gallard looked down the barrel of the rifle she was holding. The echoes of two shots were in her ears. The first had been fired by Erv Stafford. She had fired the second. Carl Oldring was lying flat on his back, motionless. Erv Stafford was lying on his face.

She thought, suddenly, "I've killed a man! I even shot him in the back. Tom wouldn't have liked that. He would have said . . ."

There were still two men in the yard, George Adsell and Chubby Quinn. They had heard her shot, had seen Erv Stafford fall and had whirled toward the house. Both had raised their guns, but she dodged quickly from the doorway. One of the two, she thought it was George, tried a shot at her, but he missed.

Myrt had borrowed the rifle from Lillian, and right now, Lillian was standing in the kitchen, wringing her hands. She looked scared to death. Myrt didn't blame her. She was frightened herself. She knew she was shaky.

What had happened had come so quickly there had been no time for thought. She had been warned they had to leave, had turned back to say goodbye to Lillian. She had not wasted any time doing that but when she returned to the back door the three Justine men were there. She had borrowed Lillian's rifle, or maybe it had been her husband's. She turned back to the door — just as Oldring had been shot. Stafford had been ready to fire another shot into Oldring's body — but he didnt get the chance. She stopped him.

200

Bill Adams shouted from the bedroom. "Hey! What's all the shooting? Where are you, Lillian? Are you all right?"

He was a sick man. It could be that he was unable to leave his bed and it seemed as though Lillian was going to stay where she was.

Myrt walked toward the bedroom. She spoke through the door. "It's me, Bill. Myrt Gallard. I'll be there in a minute, tell you what happened."

"Is Lillian all right?"

"She's fine," Myrt answered.

She crossed to the kitchen window, looked out. George Adsell and Chubby Quinn were helping Erv Stafford to his feet. He wasn't dead. She hadn't killed a man. She felt as though a heavy burden had slipped from her shoulders.

Carl Oldring was not dead, either. He moved one leg, then another. He tried to sit up, managed it.

Myrt looked at George and Chubby. They were moving away, half carrying Erv Stafford. She thought, "They won't notice me. I can go out and get Carl, bring him in here. That means we'll have to stay here — and what will Lillian say when Mr. Justine comes? What will I say?"

She had no idea what was ahead, but she knew that the first thing she had to do was look after Oldring. That was enough to worry about, right now. She headed for the back door.

CHAPTER
THIRTEEN

Arne and Fern Dillon had started toward town while it was still dark. They kept the team moving, made good time, and well before noon they pulled up in front of the general store. There, they separated briefly. Fern stopped in the store, left an order to be filled, then she visited with Cora Hopkins who ran the restaurant. She stayed there until Arne joined her. They would have dinner in the restaurant, finish what they had to do in town, and maybe they could start back to the ranch by two o'clock. Before Arne met her he would stop at the feed store, then have a beer in one of the saloons.

Fern heard what had happened this morning, at the Adams home, from Bernie Meyers. And he seemed quite concerned, worried about Myrt Gallard. Cora Hopkins was more worried about Lillian Adams, but she had said, bluntly, "I have a feeling that Lillian earned it, but I still wish it hadn't happened."

Arne found the feed store closed. He learned about the trouble from George Adsell, whom he met in the saloon. The man seemed genuinely worried. "We was after the Injun," he explained. "Someone went in the house, thought it was him but before we could say anything Myrt opened up with her rifle. Damned near

202

killed Stafford, shot him through the back when he turned away. She hit Oldring, too, some way or other. She's sort of gone crazy — grief crazy over the death of her husband. What do you do about a woman like that?"

Arne had to agree that this was quite a problem.

When Arne and Fern met at the restaurant they had different versions of what had happened. His version had come from George, who had been there when Stafford had been hurt. Fern's best information had come from Bernie Meyers, who had talked to the doctor who had attended both to Stafford and Oldring; and who had talked to Myrt, who had said, definitely, that she intended to look after Oldring. The sheriff had been to the house, to arrest Myrt, but she had greeted him with a rifle in her hands.

"She's got to be crazy," Arne said. "Backin' up that Injun, buckin' up against the sheriff."

"Red Pardee?" Fern said. "You used to like him."

"He's still an' Injun."

"Half Indian, half white."

"But the Injun side shows up at a time like this."

"Why?"

He scowled at her. "Are you backin' him up? What's the matter with you?"

"I don't like any fighting," Fern said. "Bernie told me that Mr. Justine could stop all the trouble if he wouldn't try to spread on down the valley."

"He won't," Arne said.

"What will he do if he comes to our place?"

"He might not go that far."

"But what if he does?"

"Things work out," Arne muttered. "Quit worryin' about it."

"I don't see what gives Mr. Justine the right to get bigger and bigger. I think the people fighting him have got the right to do that."

"You're talking too loud," Arne said. "People are looking at us."

"I don't care. Let 'em," Fern said.

They continued arguing, and when they left town, early, about an hour later, they were not in the best spirits. Fern was openly defending Myrt, Red Pardee, and those who were supporting them. Arne had decided that they were right in principle but wrong in what they were doing.

They headed down the road and where it climbed over a low hill and dropped out of sight of the town, a number of riders showed up and headed for the wagon.

Arne handed the reins to Fern, then he reached for his rifle. His lips had tightened, his hands were steady. "The Injun, an' some of his friends," he said gruffly. "The sheriff ought to be here."

Red, Broadwell and Fran Oldring had joined the group that had been watching the road below the Justine ranch. They had all headed toward town, but on the way they met Frank Thompson. What he told them was not encouraging. They moved nearer town, watched the roads, waited for the chance to talk to someone who might know what had happened, finally, to Oldring and Myrt. These people in the wagon might not be the first

204

to leave the town, but they were the first to leave by this road and Red wanted to talk to them.

He recognized the Dillons before they reached the wagon and he pulled up as he reached them. The others had come with him. The sight of a band like this might have seemed frightening. Red wanted to reassure the Dillons, quickly, and he said, "Don't worry about us, please. All we want is information. How is Myrt Gallard, and Carl Oldring?"

"Oldring's been shot," Arne said, and he looked toward Sally Oldring, who was with the other riders. "I don't know how bad it is. The doctor's been there."

Sally leaned forward. "Where is he?"

"At the Adams house, on Main Street. I think Myrt is there, looking after him." He looked at Fern. "Tell her what you heard."

"The sheriff went to get her — Myrt," Fern said. "He was going to arrest her but he didn't. Myrt met the sheriff with a rifle. She said she meant to stay where she was, that she intended to look after Mr. Oldring. I guess the sheriff backed off."

"Then Oldring and Myrt, both, are at the Adams house."

"Yes."

"How about Justine?"

"He's in town," Arne said. "And a good many of his men. I saw several. I talked to George Adsell. He claimed that Myrt shot Carl Oldring."

"That couldn't be true."

"Don't know about that. I'm telling you what George said. He claims Myrt is crazy."

Red nodded slowly. Then he spoke, put into words what he was thinking. "While it's light, maybe Myrt and Oldring are safe. Justine wouldn't want to attack a woman where everyone can see. After dark his men can move in. If Myrt gets hurt he can claim she did it herself. George has already told people she was acting crazy. I've got a feeling," he raised his voice, "I've got a feeling we better ride into town before it's too late."

"I'm ready," Thompson said.

"I was ready an hour ago," Andy said.

Chet nodded. Cooper nodded and Fran nodded.

"I'm going to ride in anyhow," Sally said. "Carl needs me."

Red had been thinking about this before. What would they do if they had to ride into town? What should he expect? Should they wait until dusk or should they ride in earlier? Should they all stay together, or should they go in separately, and from different directions?

Arne muttered something and Red looked at him. "What was that?"

"Justine's there," Arne said. "An' some of his men. If you ride in there's gonna be shooting. A lot of innocent people might get hurt."

"Innocent people?" Red said. "Gallard told me about innocent people, once. I mean, people who don't take a side. He told me this: "If you live in the world you've got to take part in it, stand in favor of something or take the other side. Fight for what you believe in or fight against it. If you want to be neutral, head for the

206

mountains. If you live in the world you've got to take sides."

"Haven't thought about that," Arne said. "Could be you're right. But *if* you ride into town . . ."

"I know," Red nodded. "We'll run into trouble, but I guess we're already there. What's the most direct route to the Adams home?"

"Right back up the road," Arne said. "Could be someone will see you comin'."

"Then we'll be seen," Red said. "We'll head back up the road. We'll stay together until there's some shooting. If that happens we'll split into two groups but keep riding — fast When you make it to the Adams house, pile off your horse and get inside. We'll worry about our horses later."

"Then we'll settle things right here in town," Thompson said.

"Right in town," Red answered. "The town exists for the valley. It's not the other way. This is where the trouble ought to be settled, with the town taking a stand, one way or the other."

He was thinking: "Gallard would have put it better, but this is what he would have wanted, a decision here and a quick one, before too many people got hurt."

He wheeled away, waved to the others and headed up the road toward Dry Fork. It did not occur to him to look back. If he had he would have been surprised. The Dillon wagon had turned around and was following them.

* ★ *

The sun was still high in the sky. It was pleasantly warm but Red was hardly conscious of the weather. He wondered about Oldring, how he had been hurt. He hoped he had not been badly hurt. Myrt was still with him and from what the Dillons had said, she had talked back to the sheriff, ignored his orders. Right now the sheriff was most likely puzzling about how he could satisfy Justine without being too rough with Myrt. He could be sure that Justine had prodded the sheriff to get her into the jail. Or maybe he hadn't. It could be that Justine was looking forward to the darkness.

They were getting nearer and nearer to the town. They might have been seen riding this way. Or maybe not. A reception committee might be waiting for them — out of sight. There was no one standing out in the open.

"We'll ride harder," he called to the others. "When you hit the edge of the town I want your horses to be galloping. Get to the Adams house in a hurry, and get inside. If we make it at all, we're lucky."

Maybe he was overemphasizing the importance of haste, but he doubted that. If Justine's men were in town, some would be out on the street. The moment some of those men saw them, there would be gunfire. He could count on that.

He was riding faster. He came to the first houses and he lifted his horse to a gallop. Others were pounding behind him. He saw several men down the street. They were looking this way. Then he heard someone shouting. A shot streaked past him, then another. He

208

crouched over the saddle, tore on, came to the corner of the Adams' lot and he slanted toward the house. His horse easily cleared the picket fence.

"To the back yard," he shouted. "Grab your rifles and your saddlebags. Let the horses go."

There was more shooting behind him. He rounded the house, pulled up, grabbed his rifle and the saddlebags loaded with supplies. Fran and Andy were with him. Behind them were Chet and Frank Thompson. Sally was circling the corner of the building. Red took a quick look at the back of the house. Myrt was in the open kitchen door, a wide, excited look in her eyes. She had been holding her rifle but she set it down.

Broadwell and Cooper were the last to ride into the yard, and as they dismounted, Broadwell fell, but he got up, steadied himself.

Red hurried toward him.

"Get my rifle," Broadwell said. "I can reach the house. This isn't anything but a scratch wound."

Red got the man's rifle and his saddlebags. They might need both, the rifle and the food he had been carrying. There had been no shooting since they reached the back yard.

Several of them had already moved inside. Sally had been one of the first. Myrt was no longer in the doorway. He took a quick look around the yard. Most of their horses were standing around, but they wouldn't stay here after the shooting. Someone in the town would round them up, look after them.

"You better get in here," Cooper shouted from the kitchen doorway.

Broadwell had reached the door. Cooper helped him inside. Red hurried that way. He moved inside. Two of the men were in the kitchen. The others must have moved into the front room.

Myrt came in from one of the bedrooms. She still seemed excited but she shook her head. "You shouldn't have come here. Now, what's going to happen?"

"I guess we'll settle things," Red answered.

She stopped, seemed to think about that, then she nodded. "Yes, I guess you're right."

"How's Oldring?"

"It's a shoulder wound but I think he'll be all right. He's conscious. Sally is with him."

"Isn't there another man here who is sick?"

"Bill Adams, but he is an amazing person. He told me he felt he was left out of everything, and suddenly that's not true. He's — he's in the middle of a fight. I think he loves it."

"What about his wife?"

"She's in some kind of fight with herself. Mr. Justine was here. She went out and talked to him, I was afraid she wouldn't come back, or that he wouldn't let her, but he went off without her."

"Has the sheriff been back?"

"Once. The door was locked. I warned him to leave us and he did."

"Broadwell was wounded."

"Fran is looking after him. The wound doesn't seem bad. I want you to meet Bill Adams. And Lillian."

210

"I've seen him once," Red said. "He might not remember me. Lillian knows me — I think."

She nodded. "Come on and meet Bill."

Red was thinking about Myrt as he followed her into Bill's room. She had been on the run, then she had been trapped here. She had shot a man, had defied the sheriff, and she might be facing a desperate fight, tonight, but in spite of that she seemed calm and self-possessed, not worried about anything. He had been thinking that he ought to copy Tom Gallard; it might have been more important to study Myrt. He was worried about tonight and tomorrow. Inside, he was a little shaky. Maybe he could borrow some of her courage.

"I'm not really frightened," he thought. "What worries me is that I don't know what to do next. We have to wait. We have to meet whatever happens, and things might happen awfully fast. If we had more time . . ."

That was one thing they were not going to have — extra time. When Justine moved they would hear about it. He was not the kind to wait.

Justine sat at one of the tables in the saloon. He took another drink, shook his head.

George Adsell stood above him and he seemed impatient. "I tell you, we got 'em bottled up. All we gotta do is move in."

"Too much shootin'," Justine said. "Too many people might get hurt. Are they all there? Did you count 'em?"

"Eight of 'em rode in. One was the Injun. Two was women, Oldring's wife an' daughter."

"I wish they were out of it. Where's the sheriff?"

"Still gone. Don't know where he is. Could be he's run out, but who needs him?"

"He could have been a help. If the women were out of there . . ."

"How you gonna get 'em out?"

"Talk to 'em. At least I can try it."

"You might get yourself shot."

"Not this time," Justine said.

He had another drink, stood up, and looked around. There were only a few men in the saloon. Two worked for him. There were three ranchers who lived down the valley. They had not been particularly friendly. The others who were here were townspeople. He had no idea how they felt about the present trouble.

He went outside, stared up the street. He could see the saddle shop. Beyond it was the Adams house, out of sight from here. One of his men crouched near the far corner of the saddle shop, on watch.

He shook his head, scowling. He was asking himself, "Why did they ride in? They must have known they'd be trapped, so why did they do it? If they was ready to give up maybe this was the way to do it, but that can't be it. If we could have run 'em down any place else . . ."

That was what was bothering him. This was the wrong place. Eight rode in. Myrt and Oldring made it ten. Add Lillian and her husband, that made a dozen. If they could have cornered them down the valley, whatever happened wouldn't have seemed so bad, but a fight right here in town . . .

"Goin' there now?" Adsell asked.

"In a minute."

"Want me to go with you?"

"No. Get the men together," Justine said, and he headed up the street.

He reached the saddle shop, stopped at the corner. Chubby Quinn, who was watching the house, made a negative motion. "Nothing happening, so far as I can see. The horses are driftin' away. I guess the men inside don't figure to ride away."

Justine nodded. He stood at the corner, peered toward the house — Lillian's house. How had she ever got mixed up with these people? It must have been through Myrt, It had to be that — but that was only part of the puzzle. She seemed, suddenly, to have changed. He had worked on her for weeks, then one day she gave in and he had thought that was that — but he had been wrong. He had seen her again and she wouldn't even talk to him. He had seen her today, earlier, and she had been almost defiant. How did you understand a woman like that?

He moved out in the open, headed toward the house.

Chet called a warning from near the front window. "Red! Want to talk to Justine? Here he comes."

Red had been with Bill Adams, and Lillian, but he broke away, moved into the front room.

Andy showed up. "What you gonna tell him?"

"Don't know," Red answered, and he raised his voice. "Myrt, you want to talk to Justine?"

She appeared from the kitchen. "No, you talk to him."

The man must have reached here. He called out, "Myrt! Myrt, I want to talk to you. Come on out here."

Red was still looking at Myrt. "You might be able to do better than I can."

She shook her head. "No, you talk to him."

Red nodded. He headed for the door, opened it, stepped outside.

Justine was in the yard, about three steps away from the porch. He was a heavy man, wide shouldered, and he looked tired. He didn't seem so neat as usual, his scowl was deeper, and he motioned angrily with one arm. "I said I wanted to talk to Myrt."

"She's busy," Red answered.

"Then get someone else. Anyone else."

Red shrugged, and stood there. He didn't speak.

"Dammit, did you hear me!" Justine shouted. "I said get someone out here I can talk to."

"You can talk to me," Red said.

"No, by God. But some day I'll kill you. Get someone out here."

Red shrugged — and stood there, waiting.

Justine glared at him, then he looked past him and he yelled, "Myrt! Sally Oldring. Frank Thompson, you'll do. I know you're in there. Come on out."

The front door stayed shut. No one else came out on the porch. Justine seemed to be getting more and more angry. He muttered under his breath, probably about

214

the way he was being treated, and he still refused to talk to Red. He raised his voice. "Hey, you inside! You got ten minutes to walk out. This goes for everyone. Walk out right now, an' no one will touch you. Wait more'n ten minutes, an you're dead. Understand? Dead! You won't have a chance."

There was no answer from anyone inside, at least, no answer that could be heard.

"Ten minutes, an' we move in," Justine shouted. "Ten minutes, an' you're finished. You better walk out while you can."

Red nodded. "Is that all, Justine?"

"I didn't say anything to you," the man answered. "I didn't make you any offer. You're already dead."

He spit, straight at Red, and he wheeled and stalked away. When he reached the picket fence he kicked it, but it held up. He had to step back over it.

CHAPTER
FOURTEEN

Inside the house the doors had been barred. Red, Frank Thompson and Andy were at the front room windows. Chet and Cooper were in one bedroom. Bill Adams, Lillian, and Ed Broadwell were in another. Myrt and Fran were guarding the kitchen windows. Oldring was on a mattress in the front bedroom, Sally was with him. That was the room guarded by Chet and Cooper. Broadwell, who had been wounded in the leg, insisted it was merely a scratch. He didn't seem badly hurt.

The ten minutes had passed. Nothing had happened yet.

Red checked each room. He stopped briefly to grin at Bill Adams. He was pale, thin, and he coughed almost incessantly but between coughs he had repeated what Myrt had said, that it was worthwhile to be important again, to be able to take part in something. His mattress had been dragged from the bed to a space below the bedroom window. He had a rifle and a handgun. Lillian was by his side, refusing to leave him.

In the kitchen, Myrt said, "I've started supper. Somebody had to. Lillian said it would be all right. The coffee's almost ready. We'll have eggs and bacon, and fried potatoes. Biscuits, too, and some honey. Do you know what'll happen? We might never get to eat."

"I will," Red said. "Don't you remember . . ."

Myrt smiled and she looked at Fran. "He's always hungry."

Fran started to speak but she stopped. A bullet had smashed into a window. There was another crash, and another. Justine's men were shattering the windows. The attack was under way.

Red had dropped to the floor. Myrt was on her stomach near the stove, Fran lay just beyond her.

"Stay right where you are," Red said. "Keep low, and you're not going to be hurt."

He turned and crawled to his station near one of the two front room windows. Bullets were still ripping through the house. It was not a heavy fire but it was steady. Justine's men most likely had surrounded the place. Their bullets had already broken the windows. Now, experimentally, Justine's men were exploring the rooms, fanning bullets everywhere they could. A few were hitting lower than the windows in the hope of stabbing through the walls. Some would, but everyone here was lying behind whatever extra protection they could line up in the shape of furniture. A chance bullet might hit someone but no one was greatly worried about that. This part of the attack was not very important. The big question was this: what came next? Red was not even sure what to worry about.

"This won't get 'em inside," Andy said. "Do you reckon they'll charge the house?"

Red shook his head. Justine might want it but who was going to lead it? Who would follow just behind?

He spoke slowly. "There are four women in here, but Justine's men have opened fire. There's a badly wounded man here, and a man who's dying, but that doesn't seem to worry them."

"Not at all. If Justine loses out here he ought to apply to prison for a job. He would make a good guard. They don't give a damn about anyone."

"Do you really have to go back there, Andy?"

"I could try running, but they would catch up with me." Andy shook his head. "It's hardly worth it."

The firing had slackened, stopped. There was shouting outside. Red got up, looked through the window. He was startled at what was happening. A team and wagon had pulled up the street so it was directly in line of the shooting. He could recognize the man driving the team. It was Arne Dillon; his wife was with him. Behind this wagon were two more. And now, marching along the street were some people. Not many, maybe fifteen or twenty, but most were women. They were almost to the gate.

"Those crazy, damn people," Andy said. "Somebody's going to get hurt."

Justine was yelling from somewhere. "What's the matter with you people! Don't you know what's happenin'? Get outa the way."

The people didn't stop. Those in the wagons joined them. They reached the gate to the front yard, opened it, moved in.

218

Myrt was suddenly at Red's shoulder, looking out. For some strange reason she had started crying. He heard her saying, "Wonderful! Wonderful! There's Mrs. Rodgers and Mrs. Kitterage. Effie Carson is there, and Beth Walker. Bernie Meyers from the store and Charlie Eckerman from the bank. This is their answer to Mr. Justine."

Red moved out of the way. He said, "Myrt, go out and meet them."

She nodded, but called, "Lillian! Lillian, come out here. We have some visitors — some of the people from town. I want you to welcome them."

"You mean it's all over?" Andy said.

"Yes, it's all over," Myrt said.

It would have been nice if she had been right. Maybe she was, but she even questioned it herself, after supper. Justine and his men had backed off, had left town, and it might be that there would be no more trouble. Some of the men in town were sure of it. A self-appointed committee representing the town and the valley was going to ride out to the Justine ranch, the next day, to talk things over with Justine.

"It's worthwhile doing that," Myrt said. "But Mr. Justine won't like it. Actually, I don't know what he'll do."

Red shook his head, scowling. He wanted to think that this was the end of the trouble, but he doubted it.

"We ought to ride out there ourselves," Andy said.

"I want to go myself," Cooper said. "Of course it might not do any good." He was thinking of Kathy.

219

"I'd like to settle things," Thompson said.

"That's the way I feel, too," Broadwell said. "Last we heard, Justine expected to buy my ranch, and Thompson's. Where do we stand now?"

"We wait until we hear from the committee, tomorrow," Red said. "And we stay together. The men will bunk in the barn, tonight. Maybe the women can stay inside." He looked at Lillian.

"Certainly they can stay here," Lillian said. "Bill loves the excitement. He even seems better. I know he isn't but this has been good for him."

They had gathered up their horses and put them up in the livery stable. The doctor had called again to take a look at Oldring, who had been conscious several times. The doctor was sure he would pull through. Lillian had been more friendly. She had seemed to have come to terms with her own feelings.

Soon after supper, Cooper, Chet, Thompson and Broadwell moved out to the barn, and turned in. In one of the bedrooms, Bill and Lillian were talking. The Oldrings were using the other bedroom. Myrt and Fran would bunk down in the front room, but they were still up, talking to Red and Andy.

"I wish you could stay here," Myrt said. She was looking at Andy. "I could go to Prescott, talk to the governor."

"It wouldn't do any good," Andy said. "I broke out of prison. I can go back — or I can start running. I might head for Oregon."

"That's too far away," Myrt said.

"How about Mexico? Maybe that's too close."

"I think it's worthwhile talking to the governor," Fran said. "He might listen."

"I agree with Myrt," Red said. "Take my place and my name, Andy. I'll do the running."

"I don't want *you* to run, either," Myrt said.

This had been a quiet evening, a better night than he could remember for a week. There was no gnawing sense of danger. There might be trouble ahead, but he could worry about that later. He closed his eyes, relaxed.

Myrt was talking, again. "The thing to do is this: head back to the ranch. I'm talking about me, Andy and Red. To begin with I'll have a talk with the sheriff. If he won't listen to me we'll talk to some of . . ."

She broke off, was silent, and for a moment no one else spoke.

Red opened his eyes. He looked toward Myrt, and past her, to the doorway to the kitchen. It was dark back there. The only lights anywhere in the house were here, in the front room, a lamp on the table and another lamp in a wall bracket. Both lamps were turned low but they gave sufficient light to show him who had appeared in the room. It was Ben Justine.

He had pulled off his boots, had crossed the kitchen without making a sound. He had quietly moved into the room, a gun in his right hand. It moved from side to side, to cover everyone there.

He spoke in a gruff, hushed voice. "Just stay right where you are — and don't talk." He raised his voice. "George, get in here. An' bring Chubby Quinn. Hurry it up."

Red got to his feet. He did that in spite of Justine's order. He was suddenly tensed, every muscle hardened. His breathing had picked up, his heart was beating faster. He took only a moment to regret that they had not set up a guard. They should have done that. He had known, instinctively, that the trouble was not over. He had relaxed too soon.

Myrt was sitting on the edge of her chair. Fran had straightened up; she looked pale, frightened. Andy had started to get up but he sank back into his chair. His hand was not far from his holstered gun but under a situation like this, that meant very little. Red's hand was close to his gun but he doubted that he could reach it — and he had started sweating.

Justine had edged to the side so there was room for George Adsell to move into the room. He was still wearing his boots. So was Chubby Quinn, the third man to appear. He carried two hand guns. Justine and George only carried one. Red wondered what had happened to the other riders. One, probably, was holding the horses. The others might be standing guard, outside.

Myrt spoke suddenly. "If you're going to shoot us . . ."

"Who gave you an idea like that?" Justine said, breaking in. "We just want the Injun. You sit where you are, Myrt. And you, too, Andy Gallard. I'll leave you to the sheriff."

"Nice of you to do that," Andy said dryly.

Justine pointed his gun at Red. "You're movin' out with us, Injun, but you won't be movin' far. Unbuckle your gun belt an' drop it."

222

Red moved his hands to the buckle that held the gun belt around his waist. He was thinking, "If I drop my gun I'll be finished. They'll ride me out and shoot me. If I'm going to try anything I've got to try it right here — but if I do that, Myrt could get hurt, or Fran. I've got to remember that . . ."

Andy leaned forward. "Hey you! Justine. Aren't you the man who hired Rossiter?"

"I don't know what you're talkin' about," Justine said.

"I think you do," Andy said. "Rossiter didn't have any trouble with my father. Someone hired him to come to town. Someone paid him to gun down Tom Gallard. It must have been you."

"You want to ride along with the Injun?" Justine said. "If you want to do that . . ."

"Why not?" Andy said, and he stood up.

If he meant to provoke trouble, that was what would happen. Red was sure of it, and he knew this was foolish. Andy faced not only Ben Justine. There were two other men to consider, George Adsell and Chubby Quinn. Any one was bad enough.

Red spoke quickly. "You keep out of it, Andy. The way I figure it, this is my problem. You stay here, look after Myrt."

"I was going to suggest that we all go," Myrt said.

"No, not this time," Red said.

He was still wearing his gun. He had been told to drop his gun belt but he seemed to have forgotten the order and he took a step forward.

223

"No. Stop where you are," Justine said. "George, move around behind him, get his gun."

"He better get mine," Andy said. "You better play safe."

Red moistened his lips. He could sense a warning note in Andy's voice, in his attitude. Maybe the man felt he had little chance for any future, no matter what happened. Or maybe he was thinking of his father's death and that here was Ben Justine, who had been responsible. He took a slow, steady breath and watched the three men near the kitchen door, Justine to the right, George to the left, Chubby Quinn in the doorway. Big men, but they were fast. He was thinking, "Andy will try for Justine, but he'll never reach his gun. I might not either."

George had started to edge around the room.

"Mr. Justine," Myrt said. "Mr. Justine, I think . . ."

She broke off at a sound from the side. One of the bedroom doors had opened. A man in a nightshirt had appeared. It was Bill Adams. A tall man, thin, and he shouldn't have been out of bed but he was, and he had a rifle in his hand. It was half lifted.

He called out something. It was not a shout. It was like a cry. "Justine, this is my house. You don't belong here."

He didn't aim the rifle. He just pointed it and fired.

Justine swung his gun in that direction but he never had the chance to use it. The rifle bullet hit him in the chest. It hurled his body backwards, but Bill Adams probably never saw the result of his bullet. George Adsell snapped a shot at him. Chubby Quinn did the

224

same. Both shots hit him, smashed him back into the bedroom.

That had taken only an instant but Red had needed no more time than that. He whipped up his gun, dropping to the floor. He fired at George and at Quinn, and he was getting help from Andy. George had staggered to the wall. He slid down into a sitting position, a vacant expression on his face. After a moment he rolled over on his side, as dead as the man he had worked for. Quinn had backed into the kitchen, but not far. He fell to the floor, heavily, and he made no attempt to get up.

Red took a quick look around the room. Fran seemed startled but he was sure she had not been hurt. Myrt was all right, she was getting to her feet. Andy was looking from George Adsell, to Quinn, to Justine, his gun ready if it was needed. Back in the bedroom where Bill had fallen Lillian was crying out, "Oh, no! No! No!"

"You better get in there, Myrt," Red said. "I don't think there's anything to be done unless she needs help."

He had started toward the kitchen.

"Hey, where you going?" Andy asked.

"There might be someone outside."

"Then I'm going with you."

There had been three men outside, but they didn't stay. As they tore out they fired several shots but no one was hit.

Thompson, Broadwell, Chet and Cooper hurried out from the barn, and Chet and Thompson were ready to take after them. Red voted against it. The rest of Justine's men would probably disappear on their own. There was no point in running them down. They had been hired hands. They would move on. The trouble, this time, had come to an abrupt end.

It was decided that the Oldrings would stay at the Adams house until Oldring could move back home, across the valley. That might keep them in town for two weeks. That didn't include Fran. She was going to go with Myrt, to the Gallard ranch. Red would be there. And for a time, Andy would be there. So as far as the town was concerned he had disappeared, headed off somewhere running away from the law.

"He'll have to do that, Myrt," Red said, frowning. "When it gets generally known that he's still in the valley, someone will be after him, maybe a federal marshal."

"Before then, I'm going to Prescott to see the governor," Myrt said. "Maybe that will help. I can try it, anyhow."

Thompson and Broadwell had left by stagecoach, but they would be back. They had gone after their families. Chet had gone home to make peace with his parents. They had been planning to leave the valley and he had left them — to join Red Pardee. He would not have any trouble with them. They were going to be proud of him.

Cooper was about the only one who was unsure of what he wanted to do. Kreel asked him to come back to work for him. He might do that.

226

"Why don't you go out to see Kathy," Red said.

"Hell with her," Cooper said. "I don't want to marry a ranch. It was Kathy I wanted."

"She's the same person."

"Nope. She's got a ranch on her shoulders."

"Afraid of work?"

"It ain't that! It's just — hell with it."

Red turned to Myrt. "You talk to him. If you don't get anywhere someone'll have to go after Kathy, and bring her in here."

They were still at the Adams house but they were leaving today, heading home. He went in to see Oldring. He was still a sick man but he could smile. And Sally could smile. "Take good care of my daughter."

"I'll try to," Red said, and he frowned. "Soon as I can I'm heading for the mountains. I want to go after that horse we had to let go — Night. She wants to go with me."

"I know," Sally said. "She told me so."

"You don't mind?"

"Just — be good to her, Red."

"I'll always do that."

He went outside, looked for Fran and found her. Then he didn't know what to say, so he scowled at her.

"What did I do wrong?" she asked bluntly.

"Sally said you could go to the mountains with me."

"Don't you want to?"

"We might be gone for weeks."

"I know."

"Just you and me."

"I know."

"If we just go off together people are going to talk."

"I wouldn't want that to happen, but I'm going with you."

He looked away. "Then we gotta get married."

"No reason we shouldn't. I mean, I don't mind."

He turned back toward her and he said. "I ought to be able to do this a lot better. Can I try again?"

Color had come into her face. She nodded quickly. "Try it a thousand times. Try it again and again. We are going to have plenty of time."

He remembered a little while later that he had not mentioned he was part Indian, and that at times this might be a problem. But mostly it wouldn't and sometimes it never was. For days now, with her parents, and Myrt and Andy, with Chet and Cooper, with Thompson and Broadwell, it hadn't even come up. It would bother some people but others would accept it. This was something they would just have to live with, not proudly or aggressively, but casually and as part of their life. It was a little problem. They would find others that would be much harder to handle.

"Let's go tell people," Red said.

She shrugged, nodded. "No one's going to be surprised. Things like this happen all the time."